TITAN NOVELLAS: GAMBLED & CHASED

Cristin Harber

ISBN-10: 0991647408
ISBN-13: 9780991647408

GAMBLED

ONE

Afternoon light poured through the slats of the bedroom blinds. Brock Gamble had been home alone, drunk, for days. No wife. No kids. Just him and empty bottles of Jack and Johnny.

A freight train of nausea catapulted from his soured stomach, and he stumbled into the bathroom to dry heave, which was nothing new. Collapsing to his knees, his gaze tripped over the counter. It was free of all of his wife Sarah's necessities. He twisted his head toward the bathtub, where no one had touched the bath toys he always stepped on.

His loneliness echoed around him.

Time ticked by while he climbed further into his personal hellhole. At first, this had seemed surmountable. Sarah would come home. It would blow over once he could explain. But then a week turned into two, and she didn't.

I miss her so damn much. And the kids... The pain was incomprehensible.

One bad decision had led to another. When his family had been kidnapped, he hadn't thought clearly. He'd betrayed one person after the next. His family when he hadn't utilized any of Titan Group's black ops resources. His mentor, Jared Westin, who'd taught him everything the military hadn't. His men, the Titan team that bled loyalty. And he'd betrayed Sugar, a friend who he had abducted and offered in exchange for the safe return of Sarah and the kids.

It hadn't worked. Big surprise. He'd been led around by his nuts instead of making tactical, strategic choices.

Regret hit him like a brutal tidal wave. The same wave pounded him day in, day out. As it threw another mighty punch of guilt and betrayal, Brock knew he'd throw up and pass out soon. Just to have the sandman visit him with nightmares.

Finally, crawling back to the bedroom, he stood long enough to scour the room for a liquor bottle. Something, anything, as long as it was mind-numbing.

He needed another swig, so he would either die in his sleep or, if not that lucky, be able to forget whatever dream would torture him while he slept.

•••

"Mommy." Kelly stomped in, followed closely by Jessica, who stomped just like her older sister. "Jess is copying me. She won't leave me alone. Tell her to go away."

Jessica stomped her foot exactly like Kelly had. "Jess is copying me. She won't leave me alone. Tell her to—"

"Girls, find Grandma. Tell her that you need something to do." If sibling antagonism was a sign of normalcy, Sarah's kids were going to be just fine. They'd survived an abduction and moved in with her mother, leaving her husband… who knew where her husband was. He hadn't come home, and she'd needed to get out of their house. Everywhere she looked was a memory of a life she didn't want anymore. She wasn't staying under that roof, married to a man she didn't really know. The decision was far from rational, but she'd pulled stakes and left him a note.

I never asked questions about what you did at work because I trusted you. I don't know you, and I don't know how you live with yourself.

It'd been harsh. She'd been emotional. And if she had to do it over again, she would have said something along the lines of *I can't wrap my head around Titan, and how people you work with might want to harm us. I was in shock. Still am. You promised that whatever you did at work, we'd be safe at home, and I feel betrayed, confused, and vulnerable. This isn't just about me; I have to keep our children safe.*

It wouldn't have mattered what she wrote, he hadn't been there after she'd survived a shootout. He hadn't come home to check on her, hadn't called about the kids. Sarah had known that he ran off to save the world while working with Titan. That he did things that were questionable, but he promised it was for the greater good.

So many questions. So many overwhelming emotions. And none of it was worth sticking around for if his livelihood endangered their children.

Kelly and Jessica ignored her suggestion to find Grandma and took turns mimicking each other. Maybe it was their age. At eight and six, Kelly and Jessica were like Teflon. Nothing seemed to stick, at least on the surface, though Sarah was sure she should start squirreling away money for therapy. No family walked out on a dad and remained unscathed.

It was only a matter of time before their invisible wounds surfaced.

Brock was gone for weeks at a time for work. That may've been their saving grace. The girls were used to being without him. She'd been used to time without him too. But this was different.

Every night, she cried herself to sleep because, in her heart, she loved the man she'd thought she knew. He was long gone, maybe never really existed. She'd learned more about Brock in the week living with the enemy than she had in a decade of marriage.

She'd been naïve. Purposely or not, she'd closed her mind to what he did on his work trips. When he came home with gunshot wounds or explosive burns, she *knew* it was because he'd saved someone's life. Not taken another's.

Surrounded by half-emptied boxes in her mom's Pennsylvania guest house, Sarah wondered how life in Virginia had been so... sheltered.

Her cell phone rang. She grabbed it as the girls ran outside. *Sugar.* "Hey—"

"Are you sulking or surviving?"

If there was one thing she'd learned about Sugar, it was that the woman was direct. "Surviving. Mostly."

"What about the girls?"

She stared out a window, wrapping and rewrapping a dishtowel around her hands. "They seem excited to be in a normal school. It's small, private, not overwhelming. So it's working. Much different from homeschooling them."

"What about you? You run up north, how's that going to help your problems?'

Sarah swallowed the lump in her throat. "Meaning?"

"Brock."

His name made her arm feel like stone. It fell to her side. The towel dangled, as lifeless as she felt. "You know him better than me, Sugar. Definitely in a different light."

"Bull."

She laughed sadly. Sugar never held anything back. "I miss him and wish things could've been different."

"Cut the crap, Sarah. That's the dumbest thing you've ever said to me. I was ATF. I was trained. If he was too panicked to use Titan and had to do something to save his family, I was a good bet. I'd survive. No one was taking me out like that."

"I just feel—"

"If you spout some woe-is-me shit, I'll probably come to PA and kick some sense into you. Give the guy a break."

"Excuse me?"

"Give him a chance to explain."

"You've forgiven him for what he did to you? Fine." She snapped the towel. "Well, I can't."

"That's my burden to bear, babe. He was trying to save you."

"If he'd made different choices, if I'd known the kids were in so much danger..." She turned to see if they could hear her, but Kelly and Jessica were occupied terrorizing each other. "If he'd—"

"If he did what, Sarah? I've had the same conversations with Jared. So answer that—if he'd what? Desperate men made desperate decisions. They're all morons. So you deal with it."

She couldn't stand still and stalked out of the room. "I'm angry at him."

"Hell, me too."

"You weren't married to him."

"You still are."

She bit her lip then said, "I still am."

Still, she couldn't get over her angry. It was a vicious, nonsensical circle. Like a hamster running on its wheel, once her mind started spinning, she panted through mental laps, trying to find an answer. Trying to find relief or release or resolution. But the repetition didn't help.

"Sarah," Sugar snapped. "Did you hear me?"

"What, uh… No."

"What's your plan? Sit on your ass and ponder all the ways he could've reacted better to his family being snatched?"

Maybe she shouldn't squirrel money away for her kids' therapy in the future. She should spend it now and secure her sanity, because it'd been tough on her. Sarah took pride in her self-sufficiency and a rock-solid foundation at home. Maybe that had been a lie she'd told herself, and she wasn't really strong. Maybe she was weak and pathetic but had never realized it before.

Sarah shook her head. "My plan is to move on. To protect my kids. And never feel like this again."

TWO

Brock opened his eyes to the same scene, different day. *Maybe.* He wasn't sure and didn't care. But he did know that, sooner or later, he'd have to eat. Having the shakes from alcohol withdrawal wasn't a good enough excuse to ignore the warning bells in his head. He needed to eat, and if the food stayed down, then good. If not, well then, he'd given it the old college try.

Rolling up and dangling his legs off the bed, he gathered his bearings and glared at the empty granola bar wrappers. They littered the floor. On the dresser, an empty container of peanut butter sat abandoned. A knife he'd used way too many times sat on top of an empty sleeve of bread.

Screw this. He had to eat, and with a disgusted groan, he slid off the bed and made his way to the kitchen. With each step, his stomach swished, his gag reflex jumped into action, and his ears… were now hearing sounds. Imaginary voices? Great. A new low.

There were voices in his head.

His pathetic, downward spiral was taking the scenic route. Surely, this was cosmic retribution for all of the shady work he'd done in the past, however good his intentions might have been.

Using the wall to stay upright, he pinched his eyes closed to ignore the lights and hushed away the voices.

"It's about time, Buttercup."

It took more than a second to blink. He wasn't sure if the men sitting at the table were really there.

"You need a goddamn shower."

"Christ, we should've done this a week ago."

Winters, Roman, and Rocco sat around his kitchen table, burgers in hands, and stared at him. The aroma of fast food made his mouth water and stomach turn simultaneously.

Brock had worked by their sides for years, and he'd abandoned them. Put their lives in danger. He'd done the worst thing a leader could do, and that was lie and lead them astray.

Why were they there?

They were Titan. *He* was a piece of shit, unworthy to be in the same room.

Winters kicked a chair out toward him. The loud scratching across the floor reverberated in his ears. "Sit your ass down. Before you fall and split your head."

He didn't want to. He wanted to escape from the glares and coming accusations, but Winters was right. Brock faltered forward, using the chair before he hit the floor. He tried to clear his throat, but it was too dry and abused from days of drinking and dying. "Whatever you want, get it over with."

If they were there to kill him, it'd be welcome. So why hadn't they? His blurry brain didn't care. He just wanted them out, because he had a date with a half-empty bottle of something amber-colored that sat on the counter.

Winters slapped the table. "Brock?"

"Yeah?" Brock's eyes strayed from the men to the bottle, and his mouth watered.

Roman crossed his arms and looked at Rocco. Winters ignored them all and finished his burger.

Rocco probably had Brock's job now. He'd be a natural team leader. Smart. Respected. It'd be a good fit. Titan and Rocco deserved each other. Loyal. Trustworthy. Unstoppable. *Damn it, I need a drink.*

Rocco cleared his throat. "You trying to kill yourself?"

"Yup." Why bother with a lie?

"You're doing a good job of it."

His head tilted to the side, and not because he wanted to move. It was more of a list, a weight too heavy to hold up. "Not really."

Winters crumbled the wrapper and licked his thumb. "We're not going to let you do that, fucker."

Absurd. It took a lot of energy, but Brock laughed. It came out in a garbled, scratchy cough. "Yeah, all right. Don't let me die."

Rocco shook his head. "Eat. Shower. This is your intervention, or whatever it's called."

"Whether you like it or not," Roman leaned forward on the table, "we've been a team for years, and screwing up isn't a death sentence."

Yeah, it was, actually. "It is when you've done what I've done."

"We all know what you did." Roman's intense stare burned into him. "Shit got harsh, Brock. You made a wrong decision."

"I crossed the line."

"No kidding. But we move on," Roman volleyed back.

"I don't deserve to."

Rocco downed his soda then shifted his focus back to him. "No, you don't, asshole. But that's how it's going to be."

Why did they care? "Go away."

"You have a good woman. A family none of us knew about. And no one here can say that they wouldn't lose their mind to save them either. Not Parker or Cash either."

"But Jared." Brock's head swung side-to-side, spinning. "He's a different story."

"True that. But you know who else has a fan? Sarah—in Sugar. Nicola and Mia too. And because all you fuckers are love struck and bringing girl talk into our inner circle,"—Rocco gestured to Winters and Brock—"we've got chicks gossiping. And they like Sarah. Man, we're family. Estranged at the moment, but the roots are still there. So we can't let you kill yourself."

Winters reached for another burger and threw it at him. It landed on the floor. "Brock, buddy. Eat. Get dressed. Get sober. Get your wife back and claim your life."

•••

One solid week. That was how long it took to sober up and keep down a meal.

One solid hour. That was how long Brock had sat a few houses down from his mother-in-law's house. He contemplated how badly his rehearsed speech sucked then glanced at the dashboard clock.

He gave a self-imposed deadline. One minute to pull it all together. His mother-in-law had left Sarah alone at the guest house, and the kids weren't at home either. *They were at school. What a novel concept.* Brock walked up the driveway, past the main house, to the backside of the property. The guest house loomed ahead.

The only thing he knew for certain was that his life awaited him on the other side of the door. He twisted the knob but stopped. Took his hand off and sucked down a breath and ignored the urge for a drink. Barging in wasn't the right move. Knocking was. *Knocking to see my wife. This blows.*

Two quick raps and he stood there, unsure what to do with his arms. He ran a hand over his freshly shaven jaw. Checked his hair in a reflection on a nearby window and then pocketed his fists into his jeans to keep his fingers from tapping.

The door didn't have a peep hole, and she couldn't see who was there from the front windows. The angles were all wrong. He tried to ignore how this house had little in the way of security, not that his ramped-up safety measures had kept his family from danger.

The door cracked and Sarah peered out, one big brown eye wide open. "What are you doing here?"

"Hi." His heart clutched. What *was* he doing here?

"Brock?"

He couldn't read her voice. "I'd like a chance to..." To what, explain? Justify? Beg? His mind remained blank. "Can I come in?"

She pulled back. "No."

He'd expected that. The muscles in his chest tightening and the ache in his throat, he hadn't. "Five minutes, then I'm gone."

"No." She inched the door closed but didn't click it shut.

The Sarah he knew had been bubbly and smiling. This surprised version of his wife seemed hardened. How someone could give an impression like that while only showing an eye and saying a few words, he didn't know. But he knew he couldn't leave. Not yet.

"Three minutes." How would three minutes make a difference when he couldn't string his thoughts together and—

"Fine." She swung the door wide.

He lost his thoughts again. It'd been weeks since he'd seen her. Titan missions lasted that long, but today was different, and wasn't she the most beautiful thing he'd ever set eyes on.

Her petite frame that always fit under his arm, her perfect freckles that he could map in the dark. The way her auburn hair fell over her shoulders. How familiar it always smelled, like sunshine and summer.

"Three minutes. Then it's good-bye." Nothing in her tone was sunshine or summer.

He nodded, words not coming.

Her brow pinched. "If you're coming in, then come in, Brock. Otherwise—"

"No, I'm here. Coming." He stepped through the threshold into a small living room that very much reminded him of his mother-in-law. Doilies and pristine furniture. A few cardboard boxes were flattened and leaning against a wall. The kids had toys strewn on the floor, and he'd kill to have a Barbie to step over in the middle of the night again.

The living room opened into a kitchen, and he followed Sarah to the table. A newspaper had been laid out. Pen marks and circles decorated what looked like the classifieds. Heaviness hung on his chest. *She's slipping further away from me.*

He tried to read her notes without being obvious. "What are you doing here?"

"What are you doing here?" she countered, sitting down and snagging her pen.

Sarcastic Sarah. Again, not expected. "I didn't mean…" God. Could he really not form coherent thoughts around her?

She studied him then tilted her head to the side, slowly twirling the pen. "I'm looking for a job."

"A job?"

"You know, what people do to make money? Not everyone kills and maims in order to put food on the table."

He deserved that one. Time was ticking, and he had no response. "I've missed you like crazy, angel."

Angel had just popped out. It was natural, more than saying her name, but maybe not appropriate. Too bad. She had always been his angel. Nothing had changed for him.

Her bottom lip quivered until she thinned it into a line. Sarah twirled the pen again and studied the paper. "Here's one for a preschool teacher." Her voice waivered. "I'd be perfect for that."

He took a step closer, and his arms ached to hold his wife. "Yeah, you would."

"How would you know, Brock?" Her chin jutted up, her eyes watery and wounded. "We don't know each other."

"You don't mean that." He pulled the chair out next to her. So close, but he wouldn't touch her. He shouldn't. No matter how badly he craved her. "I need to explain things to you. Be upfront whereas before I was… vague."

"Vague? Vague wasn't my problem."

"I didn't know what to do. I messed up. Bad. But it was like my world went black when you all were taken. I couldn't think. Nothing was logical. It was all survive and react."

"I never knew how close our family was to danger. Brock, you almost had another woman *killed.* That's not an environment I want to raise our children in."

She was concerned about Sugar? He wanted to shake Sarah. So what? God love Sugar. But he loved his family. His wife. There wasn't anything he wouldn't sacrifice to return them to safety. "Sugar is not your problem. And I know, from the bottom of my soul, you wouldn't care what I did if it protected Jess and Kelly. Let's boil it down to basics. Bad things happened, and I was the cause."

She looked away, and tears streamed over her cheeks. "I can't talk about this. I can't even breathe thinking about it."

He needed to wipe them away. Needed to make her hurt dissipate. But he didn't know the rules right now. Couldn't risk scaring her. "I take the blame for all of this. Things should've been different before you were taken." Guilt exploded in his gut. He threaded his fingers into his hair. "I would've done anything to bring you girls home safe. You can't see that, and I can't explain that. So just know I did what I thought was best while I was out of my mind."

She sniffled, wiping away the waterworks. "I'm not sure what to think."

The minutes were clicking by, and he hadn't said anything worth a damn. "I want my wife back. I'll spend the rest of my life making sure you feel safe again." It was rushed. Not eloquent, but there it was. The truth.

Her eyes locked on his, the look caressing him down to his soul. What he wouldn't do to kiss her right now. That was how he always felt about her. Especially when he came off the job. He needed her touch. Her kiss. Salve to the wounds she couldn't see.

Shutting her eyes, she licked her lips and refocused on him. "Three minutes are up. I think you should go."

His heart sank deep in the murky waters of abandonment. "Angel—"

"I can't do this. I can't risk the girls again."

"I can make this better. Safer. Don't take my girls from me." His voice cracked. Time was up; he needed a last plea. "Don't walk away. Not from us."

She shook her head, and he tried to remember everything Mia Winters had told him when she'd shown up shortly after her husband had left, touting her therapist card. That Sarah probably felt victimized. That she didn't understand her own feelings yet, that she needed to place blame and have an outlet. That shutting down and barricading herself were self-preservation mechanisms.

Thank God his buddy's wife was a psychologist with a major case of two-cent-itis, because Brock hadn't thought past his own feelings. He'd been content to wallow and drink.

"I love you. And I love our girls." Against all of Mia's advice, he pulled an envelope from his back pocket and slid it on top of the newspaper. "If they're okay to stay with your mom for a little bit, maybe you can take a chance with me, focus on rebuilding our family again. Rebuilding us."

Sarah rubbed the corner of the envelope. "What do you mean? What's in here?"

"Airplane tickets."

"Airplane tickets?" She yanked her hand back like the envelope had bitten her. "Why? To where?"

"A private island in the Caribbean." He took her hand, enveloping it between his palms. Her arm stiffened, but she didn't pull away. "We can, ya know, focus on you and me. We'll hash everything out in a neutral setting. Reconnect." *Neutral, reconnect.* Two buzz words Mia had used over and over.

"I don't want to reconnect."

This was the best idea he had. His go-big-or-go-home strategy, and it'd taken a lot of help from Mia. There might be simpler ways to rebuild their life other than jet-setting to a tropical getaway, but this was the one that worked best in his head. Mia said the idea was too big, and maybe he should've listened. Maybe he should listen to anyone but himself where his family was concerned, because his choices weren't working.

Brock pressed her hand in his grip, unwilling to let go and give up. "I talked to, um, somebody. A therapist. Mia Winters. She works with Titan sometimes and said this idea was too much. Too bold or aggressive. But why hold back? I've got nothing left to lose."

Sarah's bottom lip dropped open. "A therapist?"

"She also said there was stuff we could do. Talk about. Think about. Do, to work shit out." Why did talking to someone make him feel like a pussy? Such an awkward conversation, with Mia, and now Sarah. But screw it, whatever it took. He brought her knuckles to his chin, not daring to kiss them but needing their touch.

"I'm not sure..."

This was *the* most uncomfortable conversation, maybe ever. But if it had to be said, then fine. He was saying it. "We could go see a counselor, or whatever they're called. Do that once-a-week appointment thing for a few months. Or we could take off, just the two of us, for as long as it takes. I'll answer your questions. We'll make changes that work for us. Make us *us* again. Better than before."

"But..."

She wasn't saying no. That was a good thing. She hadn't reminded him that he was long past the three-minute mark. "It'd be like a second honeymoon," he urged.

She snatched her hand away.

Wrong thing to say. Honeymoons were all about flirting and screwin' and—well, he'd take that too. "Angel."

"Time to go." She stood up, nearly knocking over her chair.

Still seated, he looked at the floor, dropped his forearms to his knees, and bent over. So close, and she was backing away again. He scrubbed a hand over his face then raised his head to rake his gaze over her. That knockout was still his wife, and there wasn't a thing wrong with wanting her like he always did. Perfect breasts. Perfect hips. Pouty lips that could kiss and suck. No, nothing about the word honeymoon was off-putting to him.

Brock unfolded himself from the chair. He crossed his arms and studied. Dilated pupils. Shorter breaths. Her sharp stare dropped to the tattoos on his arm then roamed across his chest. He might not be Titan anymore, but he still had the skills to decipher the micro-emotions of a victim. Sarah wasn't reacting as a victim. Not right now. She was reacting *aroused.* Shocked, maybe at how she felt, angry that her responses betrayed her attitude. But *honeymoon* didn't scare her from him, just their conversation.

"Hell, I've missed you." The words rumbled from his chest.

She took a step back, her nipples outlined through the fabric of her shirt. "You already said that."

Springing an erection on her would be a worst-case scenario. Smart idea or not, he took a step forward. And another. Until Sarah was against the wall and he had inches to spare. "If you think packing up and moving out does anything to change my wanting you, you're crazy. Because goddamn, angel, it'd be a lie. Take your ticket. Think it over and get on the plane."

He brushed the hair off her cheek, pinning it behind an ear, and kissed her cheek. He lingered, letting his hips feel their fire, and he breathed in summer and sunshine. A nice, long breath. Just in case she didn't show and he needed something to remember.

Brock stepped back. Her eyes were closed. Her chin dropped down. His eyes traveled over her body, memorizing every swell and curve. It was her hands that would stick with him. Palms flat against the wall. Fingers splayed and flexed.

He turned, took his one ticket from the envelope, and left her alone with her thoughts.

THREE

Surprised by the tsunami of skin prickles cascading down her neck, Sarah clung to the wall long after Brock's heavy footfalls retreated out the front door. Her eyes stayed closed, still seeing him. Feeling him. Craving him.

She slid down the wall, landing in a turned-on mess. He'd always been her superhero. She'd always been his angel. Why did he have to break that out, when she had been struck so vulnerable by his very presence?

The Brock she'd married didn't run off and talk to therapists. He had all the answers. He'd known all solutions... well, until he didn't. In years of marriage, they'd had their share of fights. But he'd never been flat-out wrong. Even if she'd accused him of it. Until she and the kids had been taken.

Sarah slipped a hand over her open mouth. For all his muscles, his warrior-like toughness, he'd made himself vulnerable and asked for help. *A therapist?* It was so unlike him.

But that wasn't why she plastered herself against the wall and remained on her floor, nearly hyperventilating. His smoky, dark eyes comforted her, even if his arms hadn't. They'd seared her senseless. She couldn't help but visually trace the cording of his muscles. The colors tattooed on his arm that she knew spilled onto his back.

He was rock solid. Wide as their house. Defined tall, dark, and deadly. He'd worshipped the ground she walked on. She knew that, and seeing him was a vivid reminder. Her mind was cloudy and confused. Every time she thought of the kids' safety, she panicked. When she thought of him, she felt betrayed. But when she saw him, Brock broke through the mental barrier she'd erected for protection.

Her phone rang from on top of the table and, sitting on a lump on the floor, she decided to let it go to voice mail.

The kids!

Panic struck as her pulse hurdled erratically. She jumped to her feet. Irrational, unreasonable concern for their safety flooded her thoughts. Swiping the phone from the table, she read Nicola's name on the display. Another Titan wife she hadn't known until recently. Sarah had been cocooned in her little world, while other Titan men had loved and lived, in public. What had made Brock so scared to share them?

Catching her breath, she mentally scolded herself for thinking the worst about Kelly and Jessica. She'd come to Pennsylvania to get away from her paranoia. Like the distance would somehow help. It didn't.

The phone continued to ring, still Nicola. She answered. "Hey, girl."

"Sarah. Dang, it takes you forever to pick up. We—"

"We?" she asked, sliding into the chair Brock had just used.

"Sugar's here too."

"Hey," Sugar said. "We're in Nic's car. Speakerphone."

Sarah had briefly met Nicola but liked her. "Hey, Sugar." Since she had them on the phone and the question was fresh in her mind, Sarah used the call to her advantage. "Who's Mia Winters?"

"Good." Sugar laughed. "Brock's been there already."

"You knew?" She glared at the floor. "A little warning would've been nice."

"No, we just found out," Nicola answered. "Sugar bothered Jared, who'd been talking to Mia. Those two are chatty-Cathies, I'm telling you. Anyway, you talked to Brock?"

Talked? Not so much. Pretty much stared. Years of marriage and the man was every bit as hot as when she'd first seen him. Actually, probably hotter. He'd matured. Shed his post-military body for the hunk of steel Titan had turned him into. "Yes. Well, sort of. Wait, tell me about Mia."

Sugar jumped in. "Mia just had a baby. Winters is her husband. He never goes by Colby, but that's his first name. She's a military therapist. Deals with all those Special Forces types who can't talk about their nightmares and paranoia, helps them transition into everyday life."

Nightmares and paranoia? Sounded like her. "She talked to Brock."

"She talks to all of them," Nicola said. "Easygoing but tough as nails. If that makes sense."

"Guess so." Then again, all these Titan ladies seemed laid-back and unflappable. Just like she'd thought she was, until an abduction had proven her wrong.

"Well?" both Sugar and Nicola asked in unison.

"Well, what?"

"Don't play stupid. What'd your superhero have to say?"

Sarah's cheeks heated. She'd told Sugar that Brock was her superhero before the truth had come out. "He's not my—never mind. He talked to Mia."

"Yeah, we got that, hon. Keep going."

Sugar was the bossy one of the group, that was for sure. "They talked about how we could, I don't know. This feels so stupid to say out loud. How we could make things work again. I guess. He didn't go into details."

"He drove to Pennsylvania and didn't go into details?" Nicola scoffed. "Typical man."

"He gave me an airplane ticket."

Silence.

For a second, which Sugar broke. Big surprise. "To where?"

"I, um, haven't actually looked. It's in an envelope."

"Well, Jesus, Sarah. Go look. We'll wait."

She laughed. Yup, Sugar was definitely the bossy one. "Okay."

Why was she nervous to open the envelope? Maybe because she was considering it. The kids would be fine with her mom. They'd spent plenty of vacations with their grandma before, without her or Brock. Maybe because she didn't know how she felt about staying married, but when he was in front of her, all she could think about was the benefits of being married.

She peeled back the flap and pulled out her ticket. Leaving in two days. Flying first class. "Saint Lucia."

Nicola squealed. "Oh, I love it there!"

Sugar grumbled. "I've never been."

Laughing, Nicola added, "Well, I've never vacationed there. But I did have some downtime while playing spy games. I was able to take in a few tiki bars. All part of my cover. You wouldn't believe how international terrorists like their island getaways. But I wasn't complaining."

Sarah chewed her lip. "I've never been either." What would she bring? A swimsuit or a chastity belt? It'd be hard to focus on rebuilding a marriage if all she wanted to do was focus on his—wait. Was she considering this? And had simply seeing him been enough to start thawing her thoughts on staying married? Because she still had the same concerns. *Major* concerns. She didn't know who he really was. She needed to protect her children from the lifestyle he led.

"So, it's settled." Sugar sighed. "You and Brock are rehabbing marriage in the tropical land of luxury. If I were the romantic type, I'd think this was sweet."

It was settled? Not sure anything was settled. "I don't—"

"If Cash and I ever have a major blowout, please tell him to bring me to an island."

Major blowout? This was more than that. She'd made the decision to separate from her husband. *But* she was, at least for this phone call's sake, agreeing to give him a second chance. "I have to think about it."

Sugar made a humming noise. "Do you love the man, Sarah?"

Oh no. Now the ladies were digging in deep. She couldn't ignore them. They'd just show up on her doorstep like Brock. "Yes. I did. I mean, I don't really know who he is."

"That crap again. See, Nic, I told ya."

"Sarah." Nicola's tone was no-BS. "You can be mad at someone and still love 'em. You can hate them and still love them. Forget what he did. What you think he did. Forget it all and remember just the guy. Do you want to give him a chance?"

"Yes." She nodded. In an instant, tears welled and dropped onto the plane ticket. She'd been a sopping, crying mess. Out of character and ridiculous.

"Was he a good husband?"

"He was until—"

"Nuh-uh." Sugar stopped her.

"Forget his ways and means," Nicola continued. "In your mind, define what makes a good husband and see if he tried."

He provided for them, like he'd promised he always would. He loved her, loved the kids, without reservation. He'd never cheat. Never so much as look at another woman. He'd kill to protect his family.

She dropped the ticket onto the table. It was common vernacular. An everyday saying. *I'd kill for a bowl of ice cream. I'd kill to protect my family*. But Brock really would. And would she want it any other way?

No. She wouldn't. She knew that deep within her heart. So what was her holdup, and why was she running?

"I have to go, ladies," she whispered. Everything was clearer and more confusing than it had been before her phone had rung. "Wait, text me Mia's phone number. I want to talk to her too."

"Will do." Sarah could hear the smile in Nicola's voice.

"Send us a postcard," Sugar added before the line disconnected.

FOUR

Two days. It hadn't been enough time for Sarah. Her kids continued to be thrilled with their new school and the friends they made in the neighborhood. Her mom hadn't said much when she'd explained she was heading to Saint Lucia. But the look she gave Sarah made her feel like a teenager all over again. Her mom loved Brock. Had no idea why she'd left him and was taking his side without saying anything. Just that look. *Irritating.*

Sarah had also had two very long phone calls with Mia. After repeating several times that couple's counseling wasn't her specialty, Mia had talked about Sarah's abduction experience and the mental ramifications that came with that type of trauma.

Trauma didn't seem like the right word. *At first.* She'd thought about trauma in terms of emergency rooms. Lots of blood. Car accidents or school shootings. Major circumstances like that. But the more Mia talked, the better understanding Sarah had that trauma could be physical or emotional. There were people who'd been watching the Twin Towers fall from the safety of their living rooms, and they had mental and physical reactions, years later, when they saw low-flying planes. Mia called it post-traumatic stress disorder. PTSD.

Mia also hadn't been sure that flying to Saint Lucia was the best answer for Sarah and Brock to work out their problems, especially if there was a traumatic stress issue.

She had thought about everything Mia had said, then spent an unhealthy amount of the day on the Internet before she'd come to the unscientific determination that Mia was right. She suffered from PTSD and had to deal with it.

But also, the more Sarah analyzed her life before the abduction... *I didn't live. I just moved through the motions.*

Some days her husband was there. Some days he wasn't. Sometimes she wanted more, and other days, the complacency of life was fine.

"Final boarding call..." The overhead speaker announced her flight for the third time since she'd been in the bathroom nearest the gate, holding the sink rim and trying not to toss her breakfast.

"You can do this." She stared in the mirror and ignored the people eyeing her as they washed their hands. "Get on that plane."

She ran out the door, through a crowd of travelers to her gate. Her purse bumped under her arm, all the contents threatening to spill.

"Wait!"

Before the door shut, a flight attendant turned around, annoyed. "Almost missed us. Ticket?"

Hands shaking, she pulled the ticket out. "Here."

A quick scan of the ticket and a fake smile, and the attendant handed her ticket back. "Enjoy your flight."

•••

Brock looked out the window. The luggage had been loaded. The crew had gone through its pre-flight check. It'd been a while since he'd flown on a non-chartered flight, but the procedures were all the same. He'd been offered a pillow, a drink, then a *beverage* because apparently he looked like he needed it.

Sitting in the front row of first class, he saw every person get on the plane. None were his wife. He sank into the chair, not believing he was flying solo to paradise. First decision to make, should he drink himself back into a stupor where the Titan guys wouldn't come kick his ass, or should he fly back and try Sarah again? He pinched his eyes shut and saw her pink smile, could smell her familiar essence. A primal, possessive roar threatened to escape. Easy decision. He'd fly back and try again.

"Hi." Her soft voice pulled him to the present. "Sorry I'm late."

Angel. The pressure grinding inside melted away. She was taking a chance on him, thank God.

"Hey." He jumped up to help her to her seat, unsure what steps to take. Should he hug her? Smile? Make awkward small talk?

Sarah scooted by him, making herself small in the narrow space and clutching her purse to her chest. She collapsed into the seat and buckled in. "I almost didn't get on."

"Glad you did." Understatement of the day.

"I talked to Mia."

Alrighty, no small talk. Sarah was jumping in, and he could too. "Okay."

"I think..." She leaned over and tucked her bag under the seat and sat up, holding his gaze. She pushed her tiny shoulders back and raised her chin. "I have some traumatic stress issues to work out."

Now there's a big revelation. He saw it often with victims Titan rescued, but he never stuck around for the aftershocks. Was never part of the process after Titan declared mission accomplished. What did he say to that light bulb? Whatever it was, he sure didn't want another reaction like when he dropped *honeymoon.*

"Okay," he murmured. So much for jumping into a conversation when all he could manage was a stupid word.

She didn't seem to notice his limited vocabulary. "But there's more than traumatic fallout to work through. If we can give our relationship another chance, then I want to work on *other* things as well."

Other things? Like what? She toyed with her bottom lip. It was a familiar hesitation. There was more to come. Not entirely sure he wanted to hear it though. Seriously, there were other things to work on? News flash to him and a knock to his ego.

"I was happy, Brock. But I was complacent happy. Hot husband. Quiet life. No worries. But now I want more."

He stilled his head from a harsh welcome-to-reality shake, all shocked and defensive. She hadn't been happy? What on earth was *complacent* happy? The flight attendant who'd offered him a soda then a bourbon tinkered nearby, and he could tell she was listening. This was a very private conversation, and it was about to happen in a very public place. The other passengers felt too close. Prying eyes and ears awaited his faults not just as a protector, now also as a *husband.*

If Sarah could wait until they had the white noise of flying, that'd be his preference. His fingers wanted to tap, but his brain was pulling rank and telling him to shut up and listen. If Sarah would give him a chance, why risk losing it again? "*More.* Okay. You want more."

Her participation meant an interest in bringing his family home again. So he could man up and do *more.* He needed to know what *more* was, but he could do it. Weren't too many things in life he couldn't do. A little guidance would be necessary. *More* seemed vague. *More* was unexpected.

His collar felt tight as he swallowed a lump of uncertainty. "I'm game. But..."

"But what?" Her brown eyes narrowed.

"I think better in terms of specifics. Strategic objectives. Tactical maneuvers."

A tiny, relieved smile upturned the corners of her lips. "You're looking for a battle plan?"

Now she was speaking his language. "Actually, I had a battle plan, angel. But *more* may've just thrown me."

"You show me yours; I'll show you mine."

Every dirty thought he'd ever had about his wife came up in intense detail. Showing her goods wasn't what Sarah meant, but she never had shied away from what she wanted. *Right?* After two kids and ten-plus years together, they didn't have a problem in the bedroom. Still, it didn't keep his imagination in check.

"Brock?"

Back to the *more* conversation. "Yeah?"

"You got me on this plane, now what?"

Sharing his battle plan with the enemy was a no-go. But she wasn't the enemy. Sarah was the goal. Bringing her and the girls back home was his objective. All the details that went into his plan were mission critical. He'd need a little forgiveness and acceptance of his explanations. He agreed that she'd lobbed their marriage away because she was traumatized, not reacting clearly. Healing was needed. How upfront should he be with his tactical maneuvers?

Decision made: tell her the end goal. "I don't want to go home until I know we're really going home. Together."

The captain came over the loudspeaker, announcing they were next in line for takeoff. Brock wasn't used to the waits and delays of commercial flights. When Titan wanted to go somewhere, they'd go. If he wanted to go somewhere, he'd fly 'em. His hands itched for the control of the cockpit. In there, everything was measured and displayed. Every calculation scientific, a known reaction for every manipulation.

Sarah looked out the window as they took off then back to him. "You're assuming this will work?"

Yeah. "Maybe the same way you're not? I don't fail, angel—"

"You did." The tart words flowed over her sweet lips as her eyes hardened. "And that's why we're here."

That stung a dagger to the damn heart. He was shut down, nowhere to go, and wanted to scream, *You're alive, aren't you? The kids are safe. I didn't fail!* A restless tightness in his chest itched to escape. He might've gotten her on the plane, but her tone said that was all he had.

He and Sarah sat a million miles apart, climbing toward their cruising altitude. The therapist's voice rang in his head. *She's been wounded. You've been unavailable. For everything that went wrong, you're the scapegoat. Not that it's right, but that's probably the way she feels. You both need to heal, together. If that's really what you want.*

It was what he wanted, and even though he didn't believe he'd failed, Sarah thought so. Damn, he wasn't used to failing in her eyes and certainly not getting called for it with such anger from his wife. He swallowed his pride, ignored the pressure in his chest, and let minutes pass.

The cabin's overhead lights dimmed, and after the flight attendant offered him another drink, he turned his attention to Sarah. "Tell me about *more.*"

Her eyes bounced away from him, nervously avoiding him. She nodded and smoothed her hands over her pants. After a moment of rifling through her purse, she pulled out a purple fabric-covered book. "You have a battle plan. I have chicken scratch."

Handing it to him, her hesitancy was overpowering, and she waited, sitting still as a statue. The brightly colored suede cover showed cared-for wear, and his thumb toyed with the edges of thick paper. "What is this?"

It looked special. Treasured, and he'd never seen it before.

"Open it."

Butterflies swirled in his stomach at the secret in his hands. Since when did Sarah keep secrets from him? Probably since he'd been so open about why he'd had them live off the grid and hidden the details of what he did for a living.

Or hell, had it not been a secret? Had he just not noticed?

He opened past the first few pages, watching her expressive eyes watch him, then looked down.

His breath caught in his chest. "This isn't chicken scratch, angel."

He turned another page. More of the same. Page after page, he took in pencil-sketched scenes. Stars and mountains. Ocean waves breaking on a beachfront. Incredible detail, as if photographs had transfixed themselves from real life to sketch paper. Minute details. Powerful, purposeful smudges. Light, dark. Shading and space. It was raw, uninhibited talent.

"You drew all these?"

She nodded, a shy grin and a pink hue cast on her face.

His wife was an artist? An *extraordinary* artist. And he hadn't a clue. "I never knew."

She leaned back into her chair again, breathing out a sigh. "I know. I've kept a lot from you. Not intentionally." She looked out the window again. "I shouldn't have thrown that failure jab. Something clicks in my head, and I either shut down or lash out."

Classic PTSD. How much had she talked to Mia?

Her forearm draped over the armrest, and he took her hand, smoothing his thumb over the ridges of her balled fist.

"You've been through a lot."

Her shoulders scrunched. "I always thought I was strong."

"You are."

Sarah shook her head and laughed sadly. "I'm not. Actually, I was up all last night writing down everything I should've told you. It's toward the back of my sketch book. That's the *more.* That's what I want."

Her tight fist relaxed, but her fingers fidgeted in his hand while she shifted in her chair.

He cleared his throat. "Look…" All this honesty bullshit burned like indigestion. Didn't taste good coming up, and ignoring it didn't help. "I thought I was strong too."

Brown eyes flashed to him, ready to lob an accusation. But nothing came. *Progress?*

He continued, "I thought I was invincible. Could control the world. Guess when you can fly hot and fast, wire explosives to take out a cartel, you just assume you can save the girl. You were right, angel. I put you and the girls in danger. It killed me. Sliced my soul into pieces."

Saying it out loud hurt. Physically hurt. Stomachache. Throat ache. Headache.

"Brock… I didn't mean…"

"Whatever you meant, that's the truth."

Putting it out there, showing his ass to the universe, didn't make the aches lessen. The jet engines droned. Heavy silence blanketed them.

"Like I said, I was up all night." She stifled a yawn. "I'm going to close my eyes. But you should read what I wrote. If you want to. Maybe you'll want to write down some stuff too. It… was eye-opening."

Write down stuff? *No, thank you.* Jotting down the emo-explosion from within was a little too mamsy-pansy for him. If he did that, he'd have to queue up some new age music on his iPod and trade in his thick-as-mud black coffee for some feel-good herbal tea.

What he wanted was for his woman to fall asleep against him. She could snooze, he could page through her notes, see what *more* was, and adjust his strategy as needed.

Sarah pulled the center armrest up, and he lifted his arm for her to lean against him. But she didn't. She leaned against the window, pulled the shade down over her shoulder, and tucked her feet in where the armrest had been. Balled up, she'd positioned the absolute farthest away she could've been without switching seats.

Wrong again. His head dropped, and he ran a hand through his hair. Time to gather intelligence. The purple book held the answers.

Skipping past pictures better suited for a gallery than a sketchbook, he found the first page of notes.

My List of Secrets.

FIVE

Brock started with the section Sarah had titled *Secrets* and ended with her bulleted *Bucket List.* No way was he writing down anything comparable. First, because his self-worth as a husband had drained down the shitter, and, second, because his thoughts were all shock 'n awed.

Looking from the purple notebook to the sleeping beauty, he knew his eyebrows neared his hairline. Knew there was a perma-blush dyeing his cheeks. What he hadn't known was *his wife.*

As the jet descended, Sarah stirred. His heart clattered inside his chest. Not rhythmic. Definitely sporadic and panicked and turned-the-hell-on.

She would ask if he'd read her notebook. He could lie and say no. He could combust and say yes. Or he could just look at her the way he knew he was looking at her now, and she wouldn't have to ask the question.

His skin was crawling, burning to touch her. Be with her. Make her read aloud everything she'd penned on paper.

Fuck, man. He needed off this plane. Now.

Wheels hit the ground, and Sarah's eyes cracked open, locking on his. She didn't blink. Didn't smile. Didn't have to. "You read it."

One short chop of his head issued a confirmation.

"What'd you think?"

He blew out a hard breath, feeling too confined by the seat belt and his pants. "That we're not having this conversation in the front row of first class."

She giggled. *Giggled.* Her cheeks pinked, and goddamn, if this plane didn't get to the gate and un-board them, he was going to pull the emergency hatch.

Never. Again. Would he fly commercial. Never.

Finally, the damn door opened, and he took Sarah by the hand. She said his name, probably grabbed her purse and that notebook. He never needed to read that notebook again, every word emblazoned on his memory.

Focused solely on finding a private location, he marched them out. They were the first ones onto the runway, and he scanned the perimeter. Old habit, looking for potential threats, but right now, he mostly needed to find the quickest way inside.

"Brock," she called, keeping up with his quick pace. "Brock."

They reached inside; air conditioning bathed across his heated skin that had nothing to do with the tropics. He turned and raked a gaze over her body. Seclusion. Needed. Now.

Nowhere met his criteria. Wasn't there a flyer's club? Meeting rooms? An isolated gate with rows of empty chairs was ahead. It'd be good enough until he regrouped.

They reached the semi-insulated area, and he spun around to face the vixen he didn't know as well as he should. Brown eyes flared; flecks of copper sparkled. Her face was so familiar but suddenly so different. Long eyelashes and a tiny, heart-shaped face peered up. Lips that she licked when she was nervous, licked when she was turned on. Lips that she licked right now.

"Angel." He inhaled through his nose, trying to slow his roll. Mauling her in an airport probably wasn't high on her recover-rebuild list. His mind flashed back to her notes. Well, maybe it was. *I want us to be more spontaneous. I want the superhero to come home and take me. Nothing to do with being his wife. Everything to do with uncontrollable testosterone.*

He treaded choppy water. One wrong move and it could all end with her jabbing her finger into his chest, reminding him how he'd let them down. "Sarah. You didn't write down a lot about surviving an abduction. About feeling traumatized."

"Nope. I didn't."

Her breasts were perked, the rise and fall of her chest mirroring his. They stood inches apart, and he came closer. Hands on her shoulders, sliding down her arms, anchoring on her waist. She didn't flinch. No pulling away this time. "I'm going to say or do the wrong thing. Then you'll peel out, leaving me with a hard-on in an airport. Alone."

"I'm barely listening to you now. Don't worry about it."

Her honesty made him sway on his feet. "I can't keep my hands off you."

"Good."

"Angel. Not what I expected."

She nodded. "Think that's been the problem."

A growl rumbled in his chest. "I didn't know there was a *problem*."

"Fine." Her tongue wicked over her bottom lip again. "Wrong word."

"Tell me the right one."

"*More*," she whispered, smooth as silk.

Same word, better context. It made him growl, again. He didn't ask. Wouldn't hesitate. Not now. It'd been too long since he'd tasted her. Since he'd held her hungry little body against his.

"What changed, Sarah? You went to sleep pissed. And now..."

"And now I can't breathe for wanting you. I woke up, and your eyes were on fire. You haven't looked at me like that in years. All need. All want."

Hands still around her waist, he lifted her like she was nothing, and her fingers knotted into his hair. Her lips brushed against his, smooth and luscious. He bit the bottom one, sucked it into his mouth. Released and bit again.

Her purr danced over his mouth, followed by an enslaving slash of her tongue. The harder he kissed her, the more she gripped his hair, pulling at his scalp and driving him on. Feasting. Devouring. Ravenous. Their mouths dueled, their tongues chased. She tasted of spearmint, welcoming his intensity. Primal, elemental, she floored him. Overwhelming in a way that made a furious desire drown out their surroundings.

Her hands jerked him to her. *Hell yes, angel.* Anything she wanted. Fingernails pricked his scalp, dragging down to the back of his neck.

Clawing as he kissed her. *I thought we had a spark before. She's right. I'm wrong. We can get to more.*

Hard, peaked nipples pressed into his chest. He backed to a row of chairs, falling back with her straddling his lap. He couldn't breathe. Opened his eyes and couldn't take them off her if he wanted. They burned copper-brown, staring deeply at him. Unblinking. Unwavering.

Her lips lingered on his. Harsh breaths tangled. Their chests galloped together, his heart slamming. They could stay in this seat, locked like this, together. Not sharing a word, not needing to, and everything would be communicated.

But still... He'd said it before, he'd say it again and again until he heard it back. "I've missed you."

Sarah nodded, eyes on fire. "Hotel room?"

He hadn't expected anything this fast. "Airport and resorts are on opposite sides of the island." He cursed the logistics. "Two-hour drive. Dog-leg turns over potholes." Not sexy or fast.

"Figure something out."

Yes, ma'am. He jumped up and set her down. Lacing her fingers into his, they took off down the corridor, his erection painfully evident and pushing into his jeans. They rounded the corner and found the driver he'd arranged for with their luggage piled on a cart, ready to go.

"Where's your ride, man?" Brock stood an easy five inches over the uniformed chauffeur and pulled a wad of cash out of his pocket. "For your troubles. I need to speak with my wife. Alone. Can you take a walk? Grab some coffee? I'll find you once we've... talked."

Without batting a questioning look, the driver directed them to go out the door and to a waiting, running Hummer. Brock took her hand and led her to the vehicle, exactly where the driver said it would be.

He pulled open the door and lifted her inside. "Up and in, angel."

Sarah turned in the back seat, grabbing him by the shirt collar. "Spontaneous *and* public. You did read what I wrote."

It'd been memorized, but right now he was acting on pure, instinctive need. Public, private, didn't matter. This was them on *more*, and he liked it.

SIX

Sarah was tired of ignoring the little whispers in her head. The ones that fought for his attention while she tried to run away from him.

When she'd packed her belongings and moved out, the voices had said she needed to come to grips with what had happened, not run away from the man who'd do anything to save his family.

In the guest house, when he'd stalked close and she'd clawed the wall, those little voices had screamed for her to kiss him. Jump in his arms. Take and feel and do everything they'd been so good at while married.

And when Sarah had pushed herself, made herself write down everything she *really* wanted if they moved forward on their marriage reboot, the same little voices had given her a laundry list of feasts and exploits that she secretly dared to fantasize about but never shared.

Until today.

Now, Sarah and the sultry little voices in her head were in sync, and caveat one to staying married was to see if she could be all she wanted to be.

Brock possessed a hardcore edge to him. Brooding and dangerous. When he came home from Titan, she saw remnants of his darker side. She wanted to tap into that part of him. Now. Hormones spiked through her, traveling from her panted breaths to her womb.

She fisted his shirt tighter and pulled again. "I don't want easy."

"Wouldn't dream of it." His teeth were clenched, and he lumbered over her, closing the car door behind him.

Her thighs pushed wide open, her shorts had ridden up, pinching and pressing. The momentary pain did nothing but steel her breath, bait her for his touch. She needed this and flexed against him, trying to both alleviate and exacerbate the torturous swirls deep inside.

Her hands reached between them, found his belt clasp as he popped the button on her shorts, ratcheting her excitement up even more. They were on a mad dash. It was uncontrollable and incredible. His hands ripped up her silk shirt, pushing past the barrier of her lace bra. Never did she think they'd have sex in a car minutes after landing. But who cared? He was her husband.

Oh God. Brock's fingers cupped her breast. Massaging. Squeezing almost painfully tight. Pleasure and pain were what she craved. His fingers found her erect nipple and grazed over the tip. He teased and toyed while he loomed over her, rubbing his impressive length against her on the cramped confines of the back seat.

The man was huge. Smooth, beautiful steel. Perfect shaft. Perfect crown. He took her breath away after years of sucking, screwing, and dreaming about him.

He abandoned her nipple, snatching the fabric of her bra cups and dragging it below her breasts. Freed of their constraint, they reached for him and his head dipped. His mouth just as aggressive as his hand had been. He lavished her other mound. Biting, tormenting. Scratching his teeth over the fleshy weight until he found its center and drew her deep into his mouth.

Her body clenched. Senses roared to life, a tornado of climax building within her, traveling from nipple to clit. A sudden ambush of his fingers pushed past the lace of her thong and delved into her deeply. A welcome, violent intrusion.

"Yes," fell from her lips. Her legs spread wider as he pumped his hand. His mouth abused her tit until she catapulted, screaming, moaning, crying in ecstasy.

"More." He roared against her skin, pulled his hand free, and shucked her shorts down her legs. So fast, so abrupt the zipper scratched her thigh, and her shorts remained looped around an ankle. She pulled free the clasp of his buckle, yanked his pants down the solid slope of his ass. Hard and muscular, she dug her fingers into his flesh as he slammed into her. Pushing his cock deep inside, her body easily accepted his spear. All the way to the hilt, his sac slapped her as he entered and withdrew and pounded again.

"Fuck me, angel."

Her eyes flew open. His face pure alpha. Smoky eyes blazing. Deep concentration straining on his face. She succumbed to the all-powerful look, melted into his complete ownership. One leg wedged against the back seat, the other wrapped around his driving thighs. She met him, matched him, stroke for stroke.

They spiraled higher together. Sweat soaked, moans grinding through kisses and bites. He gripped her ass, and deeper he drove, until she was blinded with need. Unable to see anything other than the onslaught of a terrifyingly powerful climax.

It hit her more strongly than she expected. Muscles spasming. Lungs heaving. Reaching for heaven and knowing it was in her arms. He buried deep, hot seed spilling into her. Penetrating her will. Marking her as his. This was what she wanted. More than they'd ever had. More emotion. More power. More strength. It pummeled her into a heaping, uninhibited mess as she rode her wave on his shaft, coming down in a wonderful, near-painful way.

Brock collapsed, crushing and holding her. Breathing against her, into her, for her.

Tears welled in her eyes. Unexpected. "I've missed you too."

•••

Eyelids sliding closed, muscles unflexing, Brock inhaled deeply. Summer and sunshine. The woman he feared he'd lost forever, the one he still had so much to learn about after so many years together, clung to him.

He sat up, righting both their clothes, and pulled her onto his lap. "You good?" Not knowing what else to say, he figured it had to sound better than *what now?*

"Good." She made a breathy, sated sound. "That was hot."

A half grin curved up, and he gave a chuckle. "Yeah, it was, angel."

"Different."

He ducked his chin to press his lips on her forehead, letting them linger until she pulled away. "True." They'd always had fireworks, but that'd just been TNT doused in gasoline.

"You think I'm crazy?" She wasn't looking at him but out the tinted window. A cloud of uncertainty settled over her expression.

Cupping her chin, Brock drew her focus back inside. "Why would I think that?"

"Because one second, I don't want to be married anymore. The next I'm asking for this."

I bet she's totally confused right now. She probably felt erratic, bouncing from one emotion to the next. He'd practically needed a Xanax prescription after she'd walked out, but she'd been through worse, completely unprepared for it. "No, angel. Far from crazy."

"Why not?"

Reasonable question. She could be sensitive to anything he might say and react differently than either of them wanted to. But Sarah had also been upfront about her needs, and from the admittedly small pieces he knew of traumatic stress recovery, she deserved to hear how he saw the truth, even if it was handled with kid gloves.

He needed a solid minute to recover from their back-seat escape. "Give me a second."

He jumped out of the Hummer, found the driver, then returned. No telling how this talk would go, they might as well have it on the road where she wouldn't leap out and run.

The Caribbean air cleared his head, centered his goals. *Rebuild our trust, reconnect our marriage.* Moments later, she was nestled back onto his lap, their luggage safely stowed, and the Hummer was looping S-turns on a pocked road.

Where to begin? "The only reason you might be crazy is for putting up with me all these years. Imposing restrictions on our family. I've been a dick—"

"Not a dick. I easily could've questioned why and how we lived."

"But you're not crazy. Not for lashing out at me. Blaming me." He brushed a lock of her hair off her cheek. "Hurt like hell though."

The passing landscape caught her attention again, her discomfort evident. "I feel stupid. Everyone knows that I walked out. Just took the kids and left."

"Everyone being Titan?"

"And their wives."

"Trust me when I tell you, no one's calling you names. I walked away from Titan. I was disloyal. If they have something nasty to say, it'll be about me."

"I've stayed in touch with Nicola and Sugar. I think they like me."

"You're easy to like." His lips pressed a kiss to her shoulder while his heart squeezed. Of course they'd like her, and she never should've been so isolated to begin with.

She rocked a laid-back personality, always made him smile, and Sarah could run with the likes of Sugar and the Titan ladies. Not easy to do, but his wife could. No problem.

"We were so sheltered. Why didn't you ever introduce me?"

Sheltered. The word stung. Before, it'd seemed like a practical defense strategy. Now, it seemed overbearing. "Everything got complicated. Recently and quickly. All of us were single. Married to the job." He frowned, analyzing his poor rationale. "God, it's been years since Jared started Titan. When we first hit the road, mission after mission, we accomplished a lot of good, taking out a lot of bad."

She nodded as he summarized the last decade on the job.

"I met you, angel. Fell fast. Hard. You're my world, my best friend, the sexiest damn thing I've ever set eyes on. I didn't want to put a bull's-eye on your pretty little forehead. I saw bad things happen to decent people; I'd made a lot of enemies. I never wanted that for you. Sure as fuck not for our girls. It seemed safer to bubble-wrap our life. I'd be home, things would be normal. I'd be gone, you did your thing. A protected existence."

"But Nicola and Sugar? And Mia? They've got kids. I think."

"They're all new additions. It's all happened so fast. And I never thought about it. Besides, how would that go? Well, look, here's my wife. I've got one too." He rubbed a hand over his face. "That sounds ridiculous. It just never came up, and I liked you safely away from that side of me."

"That seems..." Her hand waved in the air, reaching for a lost word.

"Selfish. I see it now. What I did to protect you girls only made things worse. You're my family. And Titan's my family too." *At least they were.* "You should've been part of that. Now I've lost them and am hoping to God that I haven't lost you."

She bit her lip.

"Angel, I'm not dumb enough to think hot sex in the back of a Hummer and a revelation about PTSD will bring you home. But it'd be a lie if I said I didn't hope it did."

She scanned the back seat, finally settling back on him. Her fingers twisted in her lap. "I'm going to see a counselor about that. The PTSD." Her cheeks pinked, and he wished a serious screw could banish the negativity that came with mental blocks.

"Nothing wrong with talking to a pro. You lived through an awful experience."

"I held it together for the girls. Too many young kids in the room to let me fall apart." Her soft voice cracked. "I tried to pretend we were on vacation."

"And for that, I'm grateful. Strongest woman I know."

She scoffed. "Not really. There's a big difference between pretending to be on vacation for the kids' sake and hiding parts of myself from my husband because I didn't push myself. That's weak. I hid behind the excuse of ease."

"You thought I'd judge?" Would he have? No. Not a chance. Especially when it came down to anything in the bedroom.

"No. Not judge."

"Then what?"

"I don't know..." She shrugged. "Do you have any secrets?"

"From you? No."

Her brows bounced once, drifting down, sadly. Disappointed. "Oh."

Was the disappointment in him or herself? He didn't know. He wouldn't call what he kept private secrets. Just thoughts he hadn't shared. Which was… a secret. *Hello, genius.* "Well, that's not true. I had my own secrets, I guess."

Her eyes lit up, hopeful. "Tell me."

"I mean, I don't have some amazing talent that I've kept hidden."

She batted his chest, and it was the first time that a warm smile had crossed her lips since they'd started the drive. Secrets weren't secrets because he had something to hide. They'd just found a groove throughout years of marriage and kids. Asking for something bigger, stronger, more intense seemed unnecessary.

He wasn't any damn good at sharing. But Sarah wanted it. He exhaled heavy thoughts. This rebuilding-reconnecting stuff made for some uncomfortable moments. He rolled his shoulders and readied to flounder his way through. Only another hour and a half to kill recouping and rehashing until they reached the resort. And their private room. It had a hot tub and a private pool…

He cleared his throat and channeled his inner emotive dude. "Jokes aside. I know you wrote it all in your notebook—you've never been one to keep your mouth shut when you want something—but reading those words, knowing… this assertive thing…" Nothing he said sounded like how he felt.

But she blinked, eyes acknowledging. "I wanted something new and told you."

"Yes." *Exactly.* "Things have always been hot. I'm not complaining. Never complained. Swear." He crossed his heart.

She laughed. "I should've given you my honey-do-me-this-way list years ago." Her fingers smoothed the collar of his shirt where she'd pulled earlier. "Tell me something you want. Or like. Something that'd surprise me."

Like what? *Think.* "I like you direct. Explicit." There. That wasn't hard. Not specific, but it was fun, and he liked it. A lot.

"I want you to pick me up in a bar. One-night stand."

Remembering the notebook, he nodded. "Bucket list, action item number seven. Got that one penciled in." He squeezed around her waist, loving the change in her demeanor. "See, I'm good with specific, strategic plans."

"Seduce me. Screw me. Gimme a different name." Her voice transitioned into something sexier. A low vibration. A caressing sound. "Pretend you're meeting me all over again."

"Keep talking, angel. I'm listening."

She shook her head, tapped a finger against his pec. "Nuh-uh. Your turn."

Right. His turn. She'd had way more time to think about this, and her ideas were way more creative than anything he could come up with. "Thinking."

"Spit it out. First word that pops in mind. Now."

"Rope." *Rope*? Where had that come from? But visions of tactical rope, rappelling line, strong and sturdy, colored his sudden naked fantasy of her in bed.

"You're going to tie me up? Done. Better find a hardware store on the lovely island of Saint Lucia. Next?"

All right. This was fun. "Not my turn. You."

"You've seen my list."

"But I haven't heard it. That seductive thing going on with your voice is going to get you a round two in this back seat. Whether the driver's here or not."

She bit her lip, traced it with her tongue. "Sex tape. So next time you're on the road, I won't be by myself."

He'd read *sex tape*. But to hear her say it. Holy hell. Reality struck, and his cock jumped to attention.

Too bad he wasn't going out on a job anytime soon. Titan was done with him. Deservedly so. And he didn't want to join another team, though he craved the adrenaline fix and didn't know how to do much except for fly jets and handle C-4.

But a sex tape. He'd volunteer for sex tape duty, no questions asked. He'd volunteer this second. Her weight shifted, and he could've crawled out of his skin for wanting her so bad.

"Did I lose you?" Sarah's freckled nose wrinkled.

"No. Just thinking."

"Give me another one, Brock."

Ropes. Sex tapes. And… "Hot fudge and vanilla ice cream."

She bit his earlobe then licked down his neck. "Someone's going to have a lot of shopping to do while on vacation."

Before-Sarah was fun. More-Sarah rocked his world. "Rope and ice cream. Maybe the best things you've sent me to the store for."

The Hummer pulled up to a resort, winding to the front reception area. The concierge could hook him up. Might look twice at his shopping list, but he wasn't about to leave Sarah for long. This place was nice enough that they'd get what they asked for, no questions. And it was adults only. Surely the concierge had seen a rope, ice cream, and video camera request before?

A bellboy unloaded their bags. Brock meandered to the front desk, knowing exactly how the next few hours of their island getaway would go.

"Checking in. Reservation under Gamble."

From behind him, Sarah wrapped her arms around his torso, leaning into his back. Felt good to have her with him, relaxed and unencumbered by their recent history. He snaked his palms over her forearms, covering the clasp of her hands below his stomach.

The woman behind the counter shoved slips of paper at him. "Mr. Gamble. You've had several emergency messages left from a man named Jared Westin."

SEVEN

Brock's stomach bottomed out. Emergency phone calls? *Plural?* He knew Jared like a brother. An *estranged* brother—and that killed Brock—but nothing he could do to change that. Bet Jared was pissed Brock never answered his cell phone. But it sat at home, after not charging it for weeks.

Still standing at the reception desk, Sarah's bear-hugging arms had tensed around his torso. Last thing Brock needed was for her to freeze up and have a flashback. No telling what might be a trigger, but *Jared* and *emergency messages* sounded like it might.

She stepped to the side, eyes wide. "It can't be the kids. They're with my mom. But I'll call and double-check."

No. It wouldn't be the kids. If something had happened to his kids, Jared would've jumped on a Lear jet and beat their commercial flight to Saint Lucia. He would've told Brock face-to-face. Jared was a dick, but of the honorable type.

"I don't need to call him back." Though what circumstances would make Jared track him down and pick up the phone? Whatever. Didn't matter. Brock was here to rehash and rebuild, to make sure his wife came home again.

Her head tilted. "You can't ignore an emergency call."

"Sure I can. Dude probably's just giving me a heads up—" he cut himself off. He was going to say something about retribution, but that wouldn't help Sarah and her PTSD. "A head's up on… I don't know."

"So call him."

"Nah." Brock shook his head, pulling her close. "Nothing good will come of it, and I'm here with you. For us."

Sarah stepped to the resort counter. "I'll take the messages. He'll finish checking us in."

The girl behind the counter gave an unsure smile. Jared had probably put the fear of God in her with each phone call, and if Brock wasn't half-interested in returning the calls, she might be blamed. *Can't subject the poor girl to Boss Man's attitude.* "Fine."

A few minutes later, they were in a swank suite, and nothing about his ice cream and rope shopping list would happen anytime soon. Sarah paced. She'd checked out the room, remarked on the awesomeness of it all, but her demeanor had shifted, and screw Jared for that.

"So, you wanna..." He shrugged. Pool. Hot tub. Ice cream. Where did he want to turn the conversation when the mood had clearly been assassinated by the Titan Group's head honcho from a thousand miles away?

"Call him." She slapped her hands to her hips and jutted an adamant chin. "I'm concerned. Curious. For heaven's sake, Brock. Multiple emergency messages. Call him."

"We didn't part on the best of terms." He scrubbed his face with a hand and stared at the hotel room phone, willing it to combust. No such luck, and Sarah was right. "Fine."

He dropped onto the bed, and she joined him. Inches away, but miles in thought. Not how he thought they'd spend their first moments in bed in Saint Lucia.

"Call him," she urged again. There was that bite of her lip. Nothing aroused or excited on her face; it was pure nerves.

He pinched his eyes closed and picked up the handset. A few punches of the dial later, and Brock's international call to Titan's headquarters rang in his ear. He used a backdoor number that would connect to Jared's office. If there was an emergency, maybe the bastard wouldn't be there. Maybe, like he thought before, this was just Jared giving him a proper heads up that the time had come, and even if Brock was on vacation, Jared was gunning for him.

An unfamiliar unease made his stomach twist as Sarah stared, barely blinking. Brock wasn't one to overthink, but right now, he was. Weeks ago, everything had been so normal. Jared was his buddy. His mentor. Sarah was sweet and innocent. No reasons to check out the self-help section in the bookstore. An abduction had changed it all, and he'd never seen it coming. What was he missing now?

"Brock," Jared barked when he picked up the line. There was nothing unordinary about that, except that the tension between the two men was palpable.

"Jared."

There was a familiar heave of a burdened sigh. "I have a situation. Obvious reasons, you're the last person on the planet I'd want to call. But this cropped up fast, and I have no options. None. Except for you, asshole."

Having no choice would be the only reason Jared lasted on the line that long. He wouldn't ask for help when a trust problem existed. There must've been a red-flag issue that required differences be ignored temporarily.

"All right—" Shit, Brock almost said *Boss Man.* "Let's hear it."

Long pause. Jared never hesitated. It spoke volumes and ripped like a knife through Brock's gut. How could he have betrayed Titan? Sarah caught his eye. Easy. He'd take out anyone if he thought he was doing right by his family.

"Damn it," Jared growled. "I have no choice."

He nodded, knowing that bitch of a feeling. "Look, man. Nothing happened the way it should've happened. Sorry about that. But I'm not sorry about doing what I did, just how I did it. So if that's what you need to hear, there you go." It needed saying. Got it over with and done.

Sarah smiled at him and patted his knee. Unexpected but appreciated. He waited for Jared's response. Wondered how that would go down. Maybe Brock should say congrats on getting hitched? Sugar was perfect for Boss Man. What did it matter?

And what was he trying to do, pick up a job in Saint Lucia?

No. Not at all.

His only goal should be his wife. But a familiar adrenaline spike rushed through his system. He tried to swallow it away. Centered on Sarah, but the back of his mind called out the possibilities: There was a mark, a target, someone or something that he could take on or take out. Black ops percolated in his blood. It was a game. An urgency…

What would Brock do after they returned to the real world? Get a job at an office? Punch a timecard instead of bad dudes?

Jared cleared his throat. "There's a sex trafficker who snagged a client's teenage daughter off a beach in Barbados. We know very little about this trafficker other than his reputation—if we lose this girl today, she's a lost cause. Satellite footage suggests there's a holding compound on Saint Lucia. She'll be there less than eight hours if our intel's right, and the countdown clock is already clicking. You're her only chance."

Brock glanced at Sarah. There was no way he could say no. The things that happened in the foreign sex slave markets were enough to make a grown man vomit. He'd taken out enough freaks, rescued enough victims to know death was sometimes a better option. The answer came easy. "Done. I'm in."

Sarah's eyebrows rose. Her lips pinched together, and Brock didn't know if it was worry or anger or something more.

Jared let out a sharp breath. "Thank fuck."

"Tell me how this is going to happen."

"I've got no boots on the ground down there. Few connections, and they can only arm you on the quick. No backup. Nothing."

"Roger that."

"You get in trouble, there's nothing I can do. No way to pull you out. That has nothing to do with you and me, you and Sugar. Nothing to do with Titan. You get that?"

"I know."

"This doesn't mean we're good."

"Didn't make that assumption. I'll get that kid safe. Titan can take it from there." Because he wasn't Titan anymore. Brock's chest tightened. A sad swell of pathetic loss swirled deep in his gut.

Sarah mouthed, "Kid?"

He nodded, held up a finger to give him a minute.

"You ready for the details?"

Brock looked for pen and paper. This was the most rudimentary briefing he'd ever experienced. No satellite footage from Parker. No GPS coordinates to pinpoint locations or intelligence briefings that downloaded at the touch of a screen. He walked away from the bedside nightstand toward the desk, but the snag of the phone cord stopped him. A harsh chuckle escaped, and he shook his head. This was literally the least amount of technology he'd ever used on a rescue op. He was on a phone that had a cord, attached to a wall.

Brock motioned to the desk. "Can you hand me that pad and pen?"

She moved fast and returned to the bed. "Here."

He sank next to her, ready to take tactical notes on coral-colored paper with a sun and beach logo while Sarah stared over his shoulder. "All right. Go."

•••

Sarah listened and watched, realizing this was the closest she'd ever come to hearing her husband talk about work. Her mind raced, wondering what it could be that required multiple phone calls and referenced *a kid*.

Brock stared at his notes. She didn't make much out of it. Numbers. Maybe an address in code? Nothing that explained what their conversation meant. They'd had an unmentioned don't ask, don't tell policy. But now, watching him with his jaw muscles ticking and his forehead creased, Brock personified intensity. More than a man. Larger than life. She bit her lip, still very concerned as to what was happening and oddly interested by the idea of what terrified her.

No. She wasn't interested. That was ridiculous. If there was an emergency, bad things were happening. Someone suffered. Someone may've been hurt. Brock had said *a kid*. She'd witnessed the aftereffects from what he had sacrificed for his own kids. But never had she seen him do his job. An hour ago, he was all sex and testosterone, rolled into one hot man. Now, he was all alpha and deadly toughness, though nothing on his exterior had changed. Yet it had.

The air was charged. A prickle of dread and concern laced over her skin. She shifted, but the uncomfortable weight of the room didn't alleviate its push on her shoulders.

"Angel." He looked up, a genuinely torn expression tensed over his cheeks and eyes. His jawline remained rigid, his mouth thinned into a straight line. "I know this trip is all about you and me, and I don't expect you to get it. But I have to go out. Probably be back late tonight, maybe tomorrow."

She expected her heart to sink, expected panic to choke her, but curiosity didn't let it. "What's the emergency? You said a kid?"

"The shit that nightmares are made of. At least mine." He shook his head. "I couldn't live with myself if I said no to this job."

"Brock..." She wasn't sure what to say. It wasn't *don't go.* Because if a kid needed help, who was she to say no? And if she listened to her jumbled feelings, there was more than a smidgeon of pride. He helped people. Saved lives. Took out the bad guys.

But then the cold panic arrived, falling down her back. Just like she knew would happen. Bad guys were the problem. Not just that her husband could get hurt, or even be killed, but... dang that choking feeling of being overwhelmed. That tension and stress. She tried to swallow a dry lump, suddenly blanking on how to breathe.

Brock ran his hands over his thighs then looked out the window. The sun was setting over the water. "I have to."

He got off the bed and pulled her up and into a hug. She couldn't move her muscles. They'd turned to concrete, and she was sinking into the floor. Drowning in her concerns, her memories. But he didn't know. Maybe he'd worried about her reaction, but from his encapsulating hug, he couldn't tell that fear and anxiety had taken control of her mind and limbs.

"Angel? Sarah? You okay?"

No. She wasn't okay. But she couldn't make the words come out.

Her heart raced in a bad way, and she felt hot around her neck, her chest, her... She gasped a breath.

"Sarah?" Brock held her in outstretched arms.

Oh, no. She was going to pass out. The room tilted. Her tongue turned thick, and not moving of her own accord, she found her legs giving out and her husband putting her in a chair. He smoothed her hair, told her to breathe. Told her to look into his eyes. Focus on him.

And she did.

He was unwavering in strength. Strong, solid, and dependable.

A breath floated into her lungs. Followed by another. And another. She got the hang of it again, blinked against her reaction, her embarrassment, her unshed tears.

"I'm sorry. I didn't mean to—" Her voice broke; she couldn't finish her apology.

"No worries." He stroked her hair, smoothing it behind her ears. "I'm not going anywhere, angel. It's okay. You're my world. You and the girls. That's it."

Guilt swished the bile in her stomach. Brock had said *a kid*. She didn't want her selfish reactions or his pity. Her head shook, undoing the hairs he'd tucked off her cheeks. "But it's an emergency. With a kid."

He dropped to a crouch between her knees and stared up at her. "Don't care."

"Tell me."

"Tell you what?"

"What the emergency is."

"It's someone else's problem, angel."

His face lied to her while he tried his best to convince her with soothing words and consoling gestures.

"I'm stronger than this." She inhaled through her nose, out through her mouth, channeling every yoga video she'd ever owned. The word *kid* echoed in her head. "Tell me the emergency. What were you going to do? Where were you going to go? I'm never going to heal if I run from the challenges."

"Sarah, we're eliminating those challenges. I'm not going into the field anymore if this is what it does to you. I can't. I won't, considering what I just saw happen to my wife. Fuck no."

"What did Jared ask you to do?" Her head pounded. "Please, I need to know."

He shook his head. "Hell no. Can't do it. Let me handle the dark stuff and—"

Grasping his hands, she squeezed as much for the details as for support. "I'll assume the worst."

"You can't imagine the worst. Let it go. You don't need to know about the things I know. I want to protect you. Need to. Don't you get that?"

A swell of passion surged in her chest, materializing through her arms and fists. She pushed him back and stood up. "Stop protecting me."

"But—"

"Tell me the emergency, Brock. Tell me because I need to know. Because I want to get a handle on the tricks my mind is playing. Because we have to start somewhere, and it might as well be today. Right now."

His body went rigid. "Goddamn it." Dropping his head back, he scanned the ceiling then paced the room. "A girl, not too much older than our girls, was taken by a sex trafficker with a reputation for disappearing. Once he gets his product, the girls, they're gone. But there's a chance... a narrow window, and I can infiltrate and get her out. Not good odds, but the best the kid's got. I'd have no backup. No additional eyes, resources, no gadgets. Just some local hardware—guns—that I'd get from a third-party contact." He paced again. "That's the emergency."

This is what he did when he left home? He saved children. He interacted with scum. But he cleaned it up. She'd always known it, even if he hadn't said it outright. Not that she could've imagined the scenario he'd just spouted, but still. "That's someone's daughter."

He lifted his chin then pinched his eyes. "Yeah, someone's kid."

No way would she hold Brock back. Dangerous, yes. But if it were their girls... Sarah couldn't be the reason an innocent girl was lost to evil.

She took a deep breath. "Take me." Wait, where had that come from? But it made sense. He shouldn't be alone and just said he didn't have anyone else. Well, Brock had her. "I'll be your eyes and resources. Tell me what to do, and I can do it."

A harsh, coughing laugh answered her. His eyebrows shot up, his eyes widened. "No way, angel. Are you kidding me?"

"I won't be a liability. I won't slow you down." She took a step forward, suddenly never more sure of what she wanted. "Take me with you."

"You can't fire a gun."

"Point and pull the trigger. Seen it on TV."

"You've lost your mind." He backed up again. "The answer is no. No way. No way in the world."

She stepped to him again. "What's going to happen to that kid?"

"The kid?" Shadows darkened his smoky eyes.

"Yeah, Brock. The kid. Someone's going to buy her? Is there an auction block? Old men bidding on her? Maybe it's an online thing? I don't know how these things work. But you do."

"Sarah," he snapped. "Enough."

"What happens to her? Day one, she gets broken in by some sicko? Or does she have to wait around, terrified and having no idea what atrocious things will happen to her body?"

"Sarah! Stop it, goddamn it."

"I bet she's scared. Crying for her mom. Her daddy. Anyone to come save her. And that's you, Brock. You're the anyone. You're the savior, her superhero. Just because I freaked out, just because you and Titan parted ways, that doesn't change that you're going to save her from those inhuman predators. And I will help you, so help me God." Tears streamed down her face. "Now. What are we going to do about it?"

EIGHT

Not only was Brock passing the concierge desk without his shopping list of fun, he was doing so with his wife in tow on the way to meet a Caribbean arms-dealing friend of a friend. Far from what he wanted to be doing.

He'd never been less prepared for a meet-up in his life. He was the rule follower. The contract enforcer. Whenever Jared had an idea that skirted the line, from questionable to downright illegal, Brock always found a loophole that let them move with a little more leeway.

Now, he didn't even have a pair of tactical pants. He had on jeans, and his wife wore her longest pair of pants, white capris, and pink tennis shoes. At least he'd been able to secure a decent ride. The black Hummer sat waiting for them outside the resort's front doors.

He put his hand on the passenger door handle, not opening the door. "You sure about this?"

Sarah gave a resolute head nod. "Yes, more than sure."

Of course she was… This was an awful idea.

A yank of the door and a lift of his brunette bombshell, and he had her tucked into the passenger seat, giving Sarah her seat belt because it was about the only thing he could do to make this a safe adventure.

He jumped in and gunned it down the pocked road, swerving to miss livestock that wandered without fences and tree limbs that jutted onto the side roads he took toward their sketchy destination. Brock didn't have one weapon on him. He hadn't traveled with a sidearm. No stash of Titan accessories were packed in his bag. The only thing he'd nabbed was several steak knives from the restaurant on the way to the Hummer.

"Are you nervous?" Sarah pivoted toward him.

Nervous? No. Not a chance. He'd never been nervous a day in his life. But her little pink tennis shoe bopped on the floor board, and his gut checked his ego.

"Fuck, yes, angel. Nervous about describes how I'm feeling. I don't like this." He came to a stop in front of a shack. *That the right place?* It fit the description he was given. A short, dark-haired man stepped outside the thatched door, matching the specifics Jared had given him. Brock couldn't see the scar on his face or the dead eyes that Jared had promised, but they were at the right location. "You stay in the car."

Sarah swiveled in her chair, checking out the surrounding area. Thick, jungle vegetation. Very green. Very loud with the calls of birds and animals. The windows were darkly tinted, and no one could see in, but still, he didn't want her seen.

Aw, shit. He rubbed his temples. What was the best he could offer right now? *Honey, take a steak knife?* Christ.

"I can jump out too. I'm not scared."

She was probably terrified, but that *not scared* bit was for his sake. She attempted to comfort him. Great. Not feeling his role as a protector in any way right now.

"That's not the point. Let's keep you away from illegal arms dealers. For now." He tried for a smile. A little joke. Something to lighten his mood, maybe make her smile. But it didn't work on either account. "Lock the door. Back in a minute."

Leaving Sarah in the running Hummer, hotel steak knife in her palm, did little to alleviate the grip of anxiety in his chest. The closer he drew to his arms-dealing friend, the better he could see the scar and the eyes. The man he was meeting with was typical. Familiar, almost. The type he did business with on the regular, but the familiarity didn't change the fact that Sarah was in proximity and this whole situation didn't work well for him.

"My man," Brock greeted ole Dead Eyes.

Nothing said in return. Just a nod. Fine by Brock. *Let's do this and blow this Popsicle stand.* The shack's walls were mismatched pieces of plywood. The light came from the windows. The floor was dirt, and the table was rickety. But on that table—Brock smiled,—lay a selection of gorgeous gals. High-powered rifles. Swift-firing handguns. Gleaming with the love and care one could expect to see from a gun runner that Titan trusted.

"May I?" He gestured to the assault rifle outfitted with laser-sighting and a night vision scope.

Dead eyes nodded again, hand sweeping across the table. "The best of what I have for Titan."

It hit him like a sucker punch. Each time he thought of Titan, it left him aching. "Appreciate it."

His fingers glided over the weapon. Smooth. Solid. Brock grabbed it, ran through his check of parts and pieces. Loaded, unloaded. Tested the sight. Felt the balance. "This will work."

He selected a few smaller guns that he could tuck into his waistband and secure around his thighs and grabbed their accompanying ammo. Boxes sat next to the table. "What's in there?"

Dead Eyes nodded approval for him to lift the top. *Flashlights.* After bouncing several vague plans in Brock's head about how he'd take on a house he'd never seen and had no schematics on, he hadn't come up with much. But flashlights he could work with. He scooped several up and tucked them under his arm. "Think I'm good now."

Dead Eyes had little to say but offered him an empty box to carry his new cargo. No telling who this man was, but he'd offered the best he had, which was pretty damn good, and Brock was indebted to him.

His plan formed into more vague details as he walked to the car and saw Sarah's face shadowed in the window. What to do about Sarah. Looking into the box, Brock couldn't picture any of the firearms shooting as simply as they did on television.

He turned around, caught Dead Eyes staring. "Do you have something... defensive? Point and shoot. Nothing fancy. Very reliable."

Dead Eyes looked over Brock's shoulder, toward the Hummer. The man raised his eyebrows, tilted his head, and asked his question without saying a word.

"Yes." Brock hated to admit Sarah sat in the vehicle. But he'd left it running, and Dead Eyes, for all he lacked in conversation, didn't seem to miss a thing. "For her."

Turning on bare heels, Dead Eyes walked to the back of the shack, and Brock followed. After opening a drawer then unwrapping a cloth, his gun dealer handed Brock a simple Glock. Ten-round capacity magazine. God willing, more than Sarah would never need. Lightweight. It would fit in her palm and had a reputation for high consistency—a trustworthy weapon.

"I owe you for this one."

The corner of Dead Eyes' mouth lifted. Maybe a grin. Maybe only an acknowledgments. "Be safe."

That was the focal point of Brock's quickly expanding plan. Save his marriage. Then rescue the girl. Now, keep safe his wife.

NINE

The last crack of the fiery sun sank over the ocean as Brock maneuvered farther away from the resort portion of Saint Lucia. It'd been a long day that wasn't slowing down anytime soon. Brilliant, diamond-like stars painted the heavens, and it would've been ideal, driving down a winding road, Sarah grasping on to his hand, if they hadn't been on their way toward his definition of hell.

Brock bet Mia would say his agreeing to bring Sarah onto the job had bad news written all over it. Mia would say he shouldn't take his traumatized wife into a situation with guns and a kidnapped victim. *Anyone would say that, dumbass.* It didn't take a therapist to know this adventure might be too close to what Sarah had just survived.

"I'm a crappy husband," Brock grumbled and tried to ignore everything that Mia would say he was doing wrong.

"What? Romantic drive. Dinner under the stars." Sarah squeezed his hand. "What's not to love?"

Dinner, my ass. He snagged protein bars and Powerades from a convenience store when they gassed up the Hummer. That was before he pulled over to an abandoned area and taught her the basics of point-and-shoot. Funny thing was, she got it the first time around. Not dead-center accuracy, but she held her own with a decent position and solid grip, and she understood his strategy for their job. Sarah had asked solid questions about their maneuvers and how to handle tactical adjustments.

"So..." Sarah let go of his hand and swiveled in her chair. Her seat belt stayed on, thank God. It was still the only decent safety measure that had gone into today's plans.

"So?" Maybe she had cold feet. He could hide her somewhere near the trafficker's house. Leaving Sarah armed and sitting in a ditch was far superior to bringing her into danger. Maybe Sarah's nerves and panic were too much. He didn't want her to experience another freak-out, but he would take advantage if the situation allowed it.

"If the girls and I come home—"

He gave a quick shake of the head. "You wanna talk about that? *Now?*" His grip on the steering wheel tightened. He needed to focus on the job, on keeping Sarah safe. Then they could look toward the future.

She ignored him. "If we come home, I want to enroll the girls in a normal school like they are now. They're enjoying it and thriving."

"Glad to hear that, but this isn't the best time to discuss schools."

"Why not?"

"For one, we're here." He had driven up the road and back, pin-pointing with a decent level of certainty the coordinates mapped by the Hummer's GPS readout. "And second, you need to focus. We both do."

Sarah stared out the tinted windows. They were surrounded by thick foliage on both sides of the road. "I don't see anything."

"There should be a house down that driveway. Maybe about a half mile back."

"Oh." Her voice faltered.

Hesitation. That was his in. "Angel, why don't you stay? Sit in the driver's seat. I'll get the girl. It'll be easy. We'll come out. You'll be the getaway driver." *That sounds adventurous, right?* Sarah could get her fix, be part of the rescue op, and Brock would have a better chance of her making it home without a traumatized breakdown. Hell, he'd have a better chance of her making it home alive.

"Can it, Brock." Her arms crossed her chest. "I'm coming with you. You said you needed backup. That it'd be safer with a partner. I want to make this job safer for you. You've told me what to do, and I'm doing it. I can't hide." She glanced out the window and turned back. Her copper eyes were made of steel. "I won't. It's a deal breaker. Let me be part of this. Let me see you at work."

At work? Weeks ago, she'd had an idea of what he did but nothing concrete. Now she sat next to him, readying for an extraction. His shoulders sagged. The gravity of the evening's events weighed on his chest, suffocating him. He'd gone along with this charade long enough. "No, this isn't going to work. I can't risk you. A million things can happen."

"And you've explained how we handle those problems."

He rubbed his forehead with the back of his hand. The sweat dotting his temples had nothing to do with the island temperature. The reaction was one hundred percent nerves. "Then I won't do this job—"

"Think we've already decided that you're saving that teenager."

Holy hell, they were going to do this. "You remember our plan?"

"Yes. You recited it a hundred times before we got here."

Sitting less than half a mile from their extraction point, he would explain one hundred and one if he needed to. But she didn't give him the chance. Unclicking her seat belt, Sarah popped open her door. Brock said a prayer and lumbered out his door, feeling the weight of the Hummer resting on his back. The stakes were too high.

He met her by the trunk to arm up. Sarah held her Glock, as instructed, then took her pile of flashlights.

The black night blanketed them. They had a few thousand yards between the Hummer's location and their first assessment point. "Stay on my six."

"Six?"

"My six o'clock. Behind me."

"Behind you," she repeated. "Just like we talked about."

Yeah, he was repeating himself. She had listened. Of course she had. Sarah was smart. Sure wasn't trying to get herself killed.

They pushed through the thick foliage. Tiny insects buzzed and crawled over them as he pushed toward the house. No complaints and no reactions from Sarah as she kept pace. By the time his eyes were accustomed to the dark, they were at their assessment spot.

Brock focused the binoculars. The two-story house was impressive but locally built. That was a bonus. Nothing caught his eye that would be considered high tech in the surveillance department. A basic six-foot perimeter fence wrapped around. A few security guards wandered inside, occasionally popping outside for a smoke break, but they acted as if they were taking it easy. All in all, it was a low-key, averagely protected bunker. Brock had infiltrated hardier buildings with tighter security measures.

He wrapped his arm around her waist, pulling her close. He smeller her hair and whispered against her cheek, "Last chance, angel. Man the car? Let me do this alone?"

She must've remembered his strict instructions not to speak, and she shook her head.

Well, damn it. *Let's do this.* "I love you."

She nodded again.

All right then. She followed the rules, like he did more often than not. Time to get this mission moved into the done column.

He left her with the binoculars and checked the perimeter of the house to confirm his initial assumptions. Security was minimal. The trafficking group was relaxed, treating this house as a safe spot. *Definitely an advantage.*

Brock took Sarah's hand in his, and they maneuvered until it was time to crawl across an open lawn. At his cue, she handed him her package of flashlights and then belly crawled to a row of air conditioning units.

He moved to the front door, set a remote charge, then ducked past a side door to a hedge line. After unbundling the flashlights and then a few laser-sighted scopes, he pushed them into the bushes, using the twigs and branches to hold each in place.

They pointed toward the door, and he clicked them on. The bush was lit up, polka-dotted with white streams of flashlight and the red lasers of the scope sights. The bushes beamed at anyone who exited the side door. It looked like a lot of armed men hid in the bushes with their scopes sighted on the side door. *Good.*

A few seconds later, Brock was by Sarah's side and shoving a mixture of paper and garbage into a ventilation point. They had only a few seconds before someone saw the lights outside. "You ready?"

She gave a thumbs-up then held out one matchbook, keeping another for herself. Her fingers grazed his knuckles with the exchange. It stopped his heart and reminded him how much was on the line. But she wasn't staring doe-eyed at him. Her face was concentrated. Focused. God, he loved her.

All right. Go time. He struck the matches, lit the kindling, and kissed her cheek before running around the corner.

Time ticked by. Each nanosecond an eternity. Sarah was supposed to keep the kindling lit, stuffing more papers in when the burners turned to ash.

Smoke faintly scented the air. It would be overwhelming soon enough with those fast-burn papers, giving off a chemical smell. Brock hit the remote button for the blasting caps. The front door exploded.

Inside, yells and orders to move sounded. With the front door assumed as the breaching point, the traffickers would take defensive action initially. Anyone important would be hustled to the line of waiting cars behind the house, via the closest exit—the side door.

As expected, the side door flew open. Weapons drawn, they fired at the flashlights and scope beams, battling with the bushes. Brock watched for the girl. Watched and waited. No kidnapped girl. Only a semi-guarded man with a flak jacket haphazardly covering his chest was rushed out the door. *Must be their head honcho.* Not his mark, but damn if Brock didn't want to take the bastard out. But he couldn't do so without giving away his location.

By now, Sarah should have been safely positioned on the outskirt of the fence, ready to meet him and the teenager. Vehicles peeled down the driveway, deserting the house. Good defensive move on the trafficker's part, but bad news for his extraction target. Either the teenage girl was sold already, or she hadn't lived through the initial pickup.

He needed to double-check. Just to be certain. Even if only to report back a grim truth. Brock ducked inside, sweeping his gaze and clearing each room. No girl.

First floor. Done.

He moved fast up the stairs. No telling if the trafficker's security team had called for reinforcements or planned to drop their boss someplace safe and were regrouping to battle. Brock continued his fast inspection. Last room. He cracked the door.

The girl.

Thank God.

But why had they left her? Probably dead. No blood. No obvious sign of trauma, but she didn't move.

Her hands were cuffed to one of several metal hooks in the wall. Brock's stomach turned, knowing that, at one time or another, each hook had had a poor girl tied to it. Heaven help those girls now. But he could help this one. Working fast, he checked her. Faint pulse. Alive.

She was probably drugged. The smoky haze wouldn't help her case. He tested the ligatures around her wrists. Secure but pickable. With a few tries, he'd unfastened the locks, and her arms hung dead by her side. Brock threw her over his shoulder and ran toward the stairs.

Two steps at a time, the smoke burned his eyes. He rounded toward the side door and saw headlights flying up the driveway. Then another pair of headlights arrived.

Change of plans—he moved to the front door. The girl began to come to. The light kick of her legs turned into a full-scale thrash. She screamed, and he pulled her off his shoulder, clamping a hand over her mouth.

"I'm the good guy."

He removed his hand, but her disoriented eyes said she didn't comprehend. Hands back over her mouth, he cradled her and jumped through the remnants of the blasted front door.

Another set of headlights rolled up and parked in the yard. Problematic. They were too close to his exit strategy, but more importantly, they were parked too close to where Sarah was supposed to be.

Holding the girl to his chest, he tried again. "Everything's okay. Your parents sent me. We're getting you home."

He lifted his hand off her mouth, and she stayed quiet. Good, because he needed to check for Sarah. Fear shredded his guts as the vehicle drove into the yard, using its headlights to scan the area. It stopped, highlighting Sarah's waiting spot. *No.*

Where was she? Sweat poured down his back as Brock searched the perimeter. Two men got out of their car, walking toward—movement caught his peripheral. *Sarah!*

She had smartly moved away from the men and the headlights, but also away from an exit.

Brock focused the disoriented teenager's gaze on him. "We're moving again."

He held his rifle outstretched in one arm and picked the girl up, running them both along a wall. Searching voices floated through the night. Sarah didn't see him coming and gasped as he swooped in, pulling them all behind the protective cover of another hedge line.

Both women leaned against the thick bush, eyeing him. He put a finger to his lips and peered over the top of the bush. Every light in the house was on. The traffickers knew the girl was gone.

Another vehicle pulled up, and two dogs got out, pulling on their leashes and lurching men Brock's size around like they were playthings.

Brock dropped to his knees. "We have to go."

Angry, rabid barks howled through the house. No doubt, they were picking up the girl's scent. He had enough bullets to mow down incoming attacks but had no idea what kind of firepower the enemy housed. If Brock tipped off their location, the traffickers could easily end their night with a grenade launcher.

Sarah nodded, placing a protective arm around the girl. "Ready."

The determination in his wife's eyes made him proud, but there wasn't time for that. The teenager nodded, barely understanding her role in being saved. The dogs and their handlers returned to the backyard. Rough commands and harsh barks were way too close.

Brock moved them behind the hedges, to the fence. A click sounded as the dogs were released. Running. Howling. Barking.

If he could get the girls away, he could take out the dogs and deal with attacks. Sarah put her hands on the wall. Brock leveraged her foot up and her toss over the fence. She crashed loudly on the other side. Next up, the teenager. He did the same move and heard the same sound on the other side, but he also heard Sarah reassuring the rescued girl.

"Go!" He made sure Sarah remembered the plan.

A quick check over his shoulder showed the dogs on him. No time to aim his gun. He palmed the top of the fence and pulled up, kicking one leg—

Goddamn it!

Pain seared his leg. The attack dog bit, and razor-sharp teeth shredded into his calf. His uninjured leg kicked behind him, trying to free the steel trap of that dog's mouth. No luck, no release. He would have to pull the dog over the fence with him and—

White-hot pain clasped his other leg, spiraling from his limb into his chest. He lost his ability to breathe. His eyes and teeth clenched shut. Horrible waves of agony washed through him. The second dog's latch ground deep into his thigh. Both dogs, easily one hundred pounds each, tore into his flesh, tossing him side to side as their heads snarled and snapped.

Brock growled back at the mauling animals. He heaved himself up, carrying the two hundred pounds of canine that stayed attached. His biceps quaked. His chest thundered, but he could make it.

Both dogs released suddenly. Their retreat did nothing to ease his mangled muscles. Brock's head swam. Must be the blood loss. He grunted as he deadlifted his leg onto the wall.

Two hands grabbed the back of his shirt. *Shit.* Arms reaching for the sky, he free fell to the ground. The impact knocked his breath away, turning his world black. His legs screamed in violent pain. Brock opened his eyes and stared into the barrels of two AR-15s.

"Go!" bellowed from his lungs. He pleaded with God that Sarah was already on foot, running toward safety. "Go."

A boot kicked his temple. Stars exploded and quickly dissolved to black.

TEN

Go. Sarah had already been on the run, dragging the teenager with her, but Brock's voice somehow echoed into the night. *Go*. His voice played over and over as she slapped through island undergrowth. Branches sliced at her face, and she had no idea if they were headed toward safety. Instinct pulled her, and that was all she had to go on.

Behind her, all went silent. No more shouts. No more dogs. No more gunshots. It felt like hours had passed since Brock had yelled from the opposite side of the wall. He hadn't caught up, and in her heart, she knew that he wouldn't.

They tripped in tandem, tumbling down a hill, and came to a stop in a pile of arms and legs. Sarah jumped up then dropped. Their location was in the open. If a trafficker drove by, they'd be spotted immediately. Blood rushed in Sarah's ears, and she tried to hear past it. What would Brock do right now? He'd have some kind of plan to get to safety. Her stomach turned thinking of him, but she tried to ignore it. He probably had a plan to get to safety now. The one thing he had said was if disaster struck, she needed to get back to the resort, and he'd see her soon enough. This was definitely a disaster.

Channeling her inner superhero, Sarah resolved to do what she was tasked with. She studied the road. It looked familiar, but everything appeared the same in the dark. Taking a breath, she tried to calm down her sprinting heart. Which way to go? Right, left. Forward, backward. The girl stared at her, clearly expecting her to know what to do next. Eeny, meeny, miny, moe. Decision made. They were going right.

Crawling like she'd seen Brock do by the trafficker's house, Sarah tugged the girl behind her. They crept for miles, or at least it felt that far, and something struck her as familiar. Maybe. No, she was sure of it. "We're here. Let's go."

Pulling the girl with her, they crossed the street, crawled through a bush, and—yes, the Hummer. Sarah opened the back door, pushing them into the back seat, and slapped the lock button. Not like that would stop anyone who wanted to hurt them, but that was her first reaction. They hid on the seat, breaths bursting from erratic gulps to semi-manageable lungfuls.

"Okay?" It was all she could say.

The girl nodded.

"Me too."

Neither said another word. They waited and waited. No Brock. His voice replayed in her head. *Go!* This was a disaster, and he'd given her marching orders. But the idea of driving away from him was painful. She needed help. *No, Brock needs help, and I am his partner.* What she really needed was to keep it together. Crawling into the front seat, she found the key and turned back to the girl. "I'm Sarah."

"Bethany." Her eyes were glassy. Shell-shocked.

"Alrighty, Bethany. Let's get out of here." She turned the engine over and slammed the gas pedal to the ground. The Hummer bulldozed through brush and bush, bouncing across limbs until they bumbled back onto the road. Driving as fast as Sarah could manage with the headlights out, she gunned down the road, hitting every crack and crevice along the way.

No one had followed them. Sarah flicked on the lights after a mile and, nearly two hours later, made it to the resort side of the island. Her nerves were shot, her mind not recalling the name of their resort. All the entrances looked the same. Fancy sign. Pretty designs. It took twenty minutes of driving in circles to find the right tourist hot spot.

She turned to find Bethany slouched and asleep. "Bethany, honey, can you wake up?"

Tired eyes fluttered then shot open. Bethany panicked, struggled in her seat belt, and eyed the door for an escape.

"No, wait. Bethany. It's okay. It's me, Sarah. You're safe. Remember?" She reached for the young woman. "Take a breath. You're okay."

Bethany's eyes focused on Sarah then she whispered, "Sarah."

"That's right, honey. You ready?"

"Ready for what?"

Good question. "We have to go inside. I have to get help for my husband. You… probably want to call your folks and go back to sleep before you head home?" A sick feeling strangled Sarah's stomach. Oh, what if those were the least of Bethany's problems? Please let Brock have reached her in time. "Are you… were you… Do you need to see a doctor?"

Bethany slowly shook her head. "No. They didn't—" She closed her eyes and took a stuttering breath as tears leaked down her cheeks. "I'm not hurt. Just my wrists were scratched and my tummy hurts; they gave me something that made me sick. I just want to go home."

"I know. We'll get you there as soon as possible." Sarah watched Bethany rub tears away with the backs of her hands. "Let's go inside. We'll get you home."

How Bethany was actually supposed to leave Saint Lucia and get back to the United States, Sarah had no idea. The girl looked too fragile to put on a commercial flight, and if Titan was involved, it probably meant private jets would be used. The logistics would be answered by the same man who would bring Brock home. *Time to call Jared Westin.*

They left the Hummer, and she ignored the wayward glances from the lone bellboy and front desk girl manning the graveyard shift. Sarah's and Bethany's clothes were tattered, and their bodies were scratched. Quite the sight. Sarah led the way to her suite and opened the door. Her adrenaline had fizzled, but determination was front and center. Brock needed help, and she'd make it happen. Every other need—sleep and thirst—was secondary.

Without Sarah giving Bethany any direction, the girl crawled into bed and fell asleep immediately. Sarah sat down at the desk and stared at all of Jared's emergency messages. Each said to call, but none left a phone number.

Sugar.

Sarah jumped for her cell phone and hoped it would turn on. It'd been on airplane mode since she'd boarded the plane a day ago. No telling if it needed to charge before she could use it.

It sat at the bottom of her purse and—*bingo*—still had fifteen percent charge left. No international calling, but she could pull up her contacts and use the hotel room phone to call.

A moment later, Sarah was asking the operator to connect a call to the US, then Sugar answered on the second ring.

Her voice was sleep drenched. "Hello?"

"It's Sarah. Wake up."

Sugar's voice cleared. "You okay? It's the middle of the night. Wait. Aren't you on vacation—"

"Yeah. Was. I need Jared's help."

"Help?" The one-word question was loaded with confusion.

There wasn't enough time to explain. Simple version. "Jared asked Brock to do a job—"

Sugar sucked in a wary breath. "Jared did what?"

Come on, Sugar. Sarah kept plowing through her explanation. She really just needed Jared on the phone. "Asked Brock to do a job. To rescue a girl. She's safe. With me. But Brock's still there. I had to leave him behind."

"*What?* Hold on."

Muffled voices sounded in the background. "Sarah." Jared boomed into her ear. "You have the girl?"

"Bethany's with me. Brock's not."

"You both safe?"

"Fine, Jared." Sarah glanced at Bethany, who'd burrowed deep under the covers. "Fine enough. She wasn't hurt and wants to call her parents, but she's sleeping. Brock didn't make it home with us. They have him."

Sarah's heart screamed in her ears waiting for Jared to respond. He didn't.

"Jared!"

He cursed. "Sorry, but Brock knew the deal. I don't have anyone down there who can help."

Wrong answer. "So get someone down here."

"Sarah—"

Sugar's voice pulled Jared away from the call, but Sarah couldn't make out their conversation. Hushed, harsh whispers volleyed back and forth on the other side. Scattered sentences filtered through her earpiece. "No way." "Not alive." "Never going to happen."

Tears burned Sarah's eyes. They were talking about her husband. The one who she'd abandoned at home and then again in Saint Lucia. Her insides cramped in desperation, and the tears escaped, running down her cheeks. "Jared, please. Get him. Save him."

He sighed into the phone. "We don't have any intel. You don't even know that he was taken alive."

"How do you think I got this girl here? I was there. I saw it all, heard it all. I know he was alive because he told me to go. To save Bethany. And I did. Now it's your turn."

"You were there?"

"Yes. He needed help, and I was the only option. Now, you're the only option." She could almost see Jared shaking his head, not believing that she'd been there. "He's alive."

"*You* were—"

Really? He wants to focus on me? There wasn't time for this. "What, Jared? I'm too broken to help? Useless? Pathetic? Take your pick. But I helped Brock because he needed it. I survived, and Brock will too, so help me God."

Sugar started in on Jared again in the background. Sarah would kill to hear specifics.

Jared grumbled back to the phone. "Sarah?"

"Yes?" *Please, please.* She swallowed the apprehension choking her windpipe.

"See you in a few hours." The line went dead.

ELEVEN

Falling asleep hadn't been part of Sarah's plan, but exhaustion called the shots. She blinked her eyes open and ached. *Brock.* Then she jumped. A shadow in the sun-drenched room shifted.

Jared stood in the corner of her suite, looking out the window. "You're a light sleeper."

"You're in my room."

"Knocking's not really my style." A knock sounded. "But it is Sugar's."

He walked over and let his wife in. Bethany snored next to Sarah on the bed but didn't stir. She tucked the teenager in. "How long have you been here?"

"About ten seconds."

Sugar rolled her eyes as she waved. "He didn't knock?"

Sarah shook her head. How long had she been out? Checking the alarm clock, not that long. They'd definitely hopped a private jet and maybe even a helicopter from the airport.

Jared ignored them. "Here's how this is going to go. It's a long shot that your man's alive."

Her chest seized, but Sarah nodded.

"You and Sugar are going to get Bethany safely stowed on a waiting jet. I'll go see what there is to see about Brock. If it's good news, I'll bring him home to you. If it's not, at least you'll know."

"Jesus, babe." Sugar cocked one hip out and propped a hand on it. "Quit the dick role already."

Jared glared. "Let's not pretend this—"

"Thank you." Sarah slipped out of bed and tucked the comforter around Bethany. "I understand what happened. So, just..." Pain choked her silent.

Sugar slammed Jared with a glare. "No need to explain or apologize."

He cursed, threw Sugar a kiss, and stalked to the door. "I'll be back, with or without Brock."

•••

Back to square one. Brock was handcuffed to the wall where he had found the girl earlier. Weak-muscled and mind spent, he was content to hang by the wrists. His legs had started clotting, and the pool of blood tapered off on the floor. Between the bloody wounds stymieing into scabs and having a good feeling Sarah had safely evacuated with the victim, he would rest long enough to rejuvenate and bust ass back to the resort. Someone would have to kill him before he gave up on his rope and ice cream shopping list.

The deadbolt lock turned. *Well, so much for taking it easy.*

A well-dressed man walked in, eyeing him. It was the same man who the security team had evacuated with a flak jacket the night before.

"Glad to see you are awake." His pointy nose and beady eyes went perfectly with his French accent.

Brock shrugged. The better-than-thou attitude always irked him. "I've been in and out. Accommodations could be nicer."

"Aren't you cute?"

"My wife thinks so." *Maybe.*

The Frenchman pulled a cigarette container and gold-plated lighter from his pocket. With much fanfare, he selected a hand-rolled cigarette and lit it. Sweet tobacco burned into the air. "You stole from me."

Brock squinted one eye and tilted his head, sarcastically considering what the man had said. "I returned something that wasn't yours to take."

The man rolled his cigarette between his thumb and forefinger. "You have quite the attitude for a bleeding man tied to a hook."

"I've made a lot of bad decisions lately. Starting to think I shouldn't trust my own judgment."

The Frenchman took a long drag and let the smoke waft out his mouth while he paced the tiny room. "Interesting."

He shrugged. "Not really."

"I agree."

Brock laughed and dropped his gaze. "Fucker."

Polished shoes stopped pacing by his busted calf. He knew what would come next. Bad news was always so predictable. But the pain still exploded when the Frenchman reared back his toe and punted into his leg. Vicious torment shot up his thigh and down to his toes. Brock grunted, absorbing the impact.

"Tough man," Frenchie sneered.

"Just another day in the life of me." Brock gritted his teeth together. "Each one getting better than the last."

"Explain to me why one man freed my girl?"

"Seemed like the right thing to do. You sickos have messed with enough kids. My day would be a better day if someone took you out. Penance for making the world a worse place."

"Ah, and I think the same about you." Smoke encircled the man's head. "I hate losing my merchandise."

Brock's brow pinched, and his molars ground. "She's a kid, asshole."

"She was my product. Hand-selected, I'll have you know. That young woman met very specific criteria I'd been searching for. And for losing her, you will pay."

Anger boiled under Brock's skin. "Nothing about that kid was a woman. Get over yourself."

Frenchie took a small pistol from his pocket. It was gold-plated and matched the lighter.

Of course. Brock chuckled. "We going to do this now? You're just going to blow my brains out with your fancy one-shot?"

"There is always something distasteful about Americans." Frenchie paced the room again then stopped and ashed his cigarette over Brock's leg. "But you don't seem to care about your life."

He pretended not to care, but it gave him an idea. "Gimme a smoke and let's do get it over with. I'm not into big, drawn-out ordeals."

Frenchie laughed. "Very well. A cigarette, and that will be that. Certainly won't miss all the crying and pleading that comes with this part of the job."

Brock dropped his shoulders like a defeated pussy. *Dumbass.* Frenchie removed a set of keys from his pocket and reached for Brock's handcuffs. His hands dropped; pins and needles tingled from his fingertips to elbows. He rolled his wrists and massaged his fingers then rubbed his eyes, playing the part of a dead man walking. Well, dead man sitting, readying to smoke his final cigarette. *I hate cigarettes.*

The Frenchman held the hand-rolled tobacco toward Brock. He accepted, wrinkling his forehead and letting his shoulders hang even more despondently. "At least I got the girl."

"Whatever, as you Americans say. Seems that would be the least of your concerns."

Brock's head rolled, and he eyed the door behind Frenchie, then pathetically prattled about how he'd lived his life with honor. The cigarette stuck to Brock's lip, and he let it hang until the Frenchman bent over with the lighter. Brock inhaled, savoring the disgusting burn, smiling with appreciation toward his captor. "*Merci.*"

Frenchie's beady eyes pinched and acknowledged the thank you.

Brock sucked down another gag-inducing drag of the cigarette. The long embers reddened and burned. Smoke wafted around his head, sliding out his mouth as he let a sickening, relaxed exhale set his mood. Contemplative. Ready to meet his maker.

Frenchie seemed to appreciate the need for the nicotine. His guard was down, and Brock was in prime position. In a flash, he blew the smoke out hard, threw the long end of the cigarette into Frenchie's eyes, and followed with a right hook to the jaw.

An eruption of pain traveled through Brock's legs. The pistol skittered across the room. He lunged across the floor. His fresh scabs roared, stinging and throbbing pain. Nauseous from the pain and nicotine, he swallowed a threatening dry heave and snagged the pistol off the floor. A quick look over his shoulder, and he cocked the fancy hammer and let the engraved, plated pistol explode at point-blank range.

Frenchie had been mid-rebound. Arms outstretched, he'd been throwing himself toward the gun also. But momentum stopped. Blood splattered. The blast echoed in the tiny room.

Whoever else was in the house surely heard the blast. *Time to move.* Brock checked Frenchie for additional firepower but came up empty-handed. He rolled off the floor, staggering to the wall and to the door. Brilliant agony pierced his breaths. Each struggling step sent shards of pain cutting through his veins. Gritting his teeth until his jaw could crack, Brock sweated each miserable move.

The deadbolt was unlocked, and he dragged himself out the door with the pansy-assed pistol in hand. No one rushed up the stairs. *Guess shooting inside didn't break any house rules.* But if Frenchie didn't appear soon, it would probably raise some eyebrows. Brock had to get out fast. Too bad nothing about his leg injuries made fast easy.

Slinking down one god-awful step at a time, he thought about Sarah. About his girls. Brock would make it home, no questions asked. He'd make them a new life. Whatever Sarah wanted. New school? No problem. A job? If she wanted one, it was hers to figure out. She could redecorate, re-wardrobe, re-anything. If she wanted *more*, he would figure out a way to support them. Whatever they wanted in life.

Cheering men stole him away from his pain-numbing thoughts. But had there been another noise? Brock peered through a banister rail. No men in sight. Scooting down the remainder of the stairs, he listened to the trafficker's men in the parlor. Soccer broadcast loudly on a television and no one reacted to the other sound Brock was sure he had heard.

Ideally, he could snag keys to one of the Jeeps sitting outside and make his getaway. Considering how much blood loss and festering infection he had, that would be the perfect solution. But the SUVs were parked out a window and within eyeshot. He couldn't waste time hot-wiring. *Find keys.* He could do a quick recon, but if nothing turned up, he'd have better luck slipping off the property on foot. There was always another way to find transportation.

Brock crept pass the now-boarded-up front door and headed to the kitchen. Kitchen counters were the universal landing zones for keys, right? But he'd have to pass the threshold to the parlor.

The soccer game caused a round of boos, and he made his move. As if his prayers had been answered, a pile of keys was strewn on the counter. He pocketed all the keys. No need for anyone else to have transportation. Too bad there wasn't a cache of weapons sitting on the table along with a bottle of water and a burger.

He maneuvered out of the kitchen, listening for the soccer game to give him cover. A footstep creaked on the stairs, and he pushed against the wall, unable to see who was coming. Brock's eyes dropped to a blood-smeared wall. *Shit.* The reddish marks were a telltale sign that he wasn't handcuffed to a wall anymore.

Another step on the stairs. Soft. Nearly a figment of his imagination, but he trusted his instincts and stayed against the wall.

Click.

The din wasn't the hammer of a gun, readying to fire. Nor was it an electronic switching off. The click was a familiar, radio-silence sound. A soft tut meant to share information or gain attention. Brock took a step, uncertainty scratching at his thoughts.

What the hell?

TWELVE

Brock's jaw fell. Jared stood midway up the stairs. He was the last person on earth Brock expected. By the furrowed brow and nasty glare, he could tell Boss Man wanted to be in Saint Lucia about as much as Brock had wanted Sarah on an extraction operation.

A quick exchange of familiar hand gestures, and Jared traversed down the stairs and met Brock against the wall.

"Hey, asshole."

"Boss Man." It came out automatically and hit Brock in the gut so hard he flinched. "Jared."

Jared nodded. "You can thank your wife."

"She's a keeper." *As long as she'll stay married.*

They exchanged a rundown of intel and passed the parlor during an eruption of soccer cheers. They pushed out the side door. Brock pulled out a set of keys, hit the unlock button to see which set of headlights would flash. There were Jeeps along the side and back of the house, and Jared caught sight of the flashing lights and pointed.

They ducked and ran to the Jeep. Brock jumped into the driver's seat, and he turned the ignition as Jared shut the passenger door. They flew down the driveway while Jared directed him to his stashed vehicle. No telling if the Jeep had a tracking device or was rigged to blow. They needed to ditch it as soon as they were clear.

Brock kept the pedal pushed to the floorboard until the road ended. They jumped out and ran through the underbrush until Jared flagged him to stop. A Range Rover was covered netting and branches, and they peeled the camouflage off of it. Another minute later, they had jumped in and were rolling down a hill before they finally bounced onto a road.

Awkward silence hung between them. Brock's legs throbbed. He was covered in sweat and could smell the stench of his dried blood.

His throat was dry, and he needed to tend to his legs. "Got a first aid kit in this rig?"

"Nothing worth your time. But it's in the back."

Brock reached over and found it tucked behind his seat. The contents sucked. A few bandages, couple tubes of ointments, and smelling salts. A few bottles of water rolled on the floor, and he cracked one open. Finishing it in a couple gulps, he grabbed another one then peeled his shredded pants legs back.

The torn skin was red and swollen. He needed a shot of antibiotics and a whole lot of antibacterial cream.

"When you get a sec, pull over. I gotta douse my legs."

"Roger that."

A few miles ahead, Jared pulled into a decent defensive position, and Brock opened his door. Tearing the pants legs into shorts, he washed his shredded skin down and smeared the ointment tubes over the worst of his wounds. Hot fire scored across the cuts, and his breaths labored. Each leg pulsed. Brock had enough of a medical background that he knew a doctor was needed on the quick. He shook it off and crawled back into his seat.

Jared gave him a once-over. "What the hell happened?"

"Dogs."

He nodded and gave a knowing laugh. "Hate attack dogs."

"At least the girls got out. The kid's going to be okay? Sarah's good?"

"The kid's good. Considering. Your wife's bossy. Pretty much grabbed me by the nuts and dragged me here."

Brock chuckled. Jared had a soft spot for direct women who made demands. "Guess I owe her for that."

"Yup. You do."

Because Boss Man wouldn't have come for me if it hadn't been for Sarah. He could've gotten out, but the job had been a lot easier after Jared arrived with his vehicle. "This is going to be an awkward drive back."

"Yup." Jared cracked his knuckles. "Thanks for the kid though."

"Yeah. No problem."

Miles passed as they curved around the island road. Brock checked the dashboard clock. *Great. Fifteen minutes have passed.*

Jared cleared his throat. "So the guys said you've been a mess. Trying to kill yourself with the bottle. Sugar said Sarah left you."

"Sounds about right. Thanks for the recap." *Jackass.* He swallowed away the desire for a strong drink and cracked another bottle of water instead.

"I wanted you dead," Jared grumbled.

"I don't blame you, but I had my reasons."

Jared yanked the steering wheel. The Rover came to a hard stop on a sandy shoulder. He leaned across the confines of the car, pointing his finger into Brock's chest. "You screwed up, man. You are the rule follower. You know the right move when everyone around you wants to make the wrong one. What happened to you?"

"Christ, man." Brock scrubbed his hands into his hair. "What do you want from me?"

"A goddamn explanation."

"Simple. My family was in danger. Nothing would stop me. It spiraled out of control. I hate how it went down. But there's the test of loyalty. Pit my family against Titan, and my family wins. I didn't question it."

Jared snarled at him. "I didn't even know you had a wife and kids. My second-in-command, the dude I've worked with for more than a decade, didn't trust me with that kind of intel?"

"Seemed safer that way." *I was wrong though.*

"You're a moron."

Brock checked the clock again. Only another hour and thirty minutes until they were back at the resort. He shifted in his seat, and his legs throbbed.

"But Sugar's got a different take than I do," Jared grumbled.

"She's got a different take on life." What was there to say? *Glad you married the woman I almost killed. Sorry I abducted your now-wife.*

"Yeah." Jared's knuckles pinked as he strangled the steering wheel. "You want to know what she says?"

"Not really."

"Don't blame you. That woman's a ballbuster." Jared laughed. Real and honest. "But she doesn't think you should be dead."

Not what Brock expected. "Why?"

"No idea. Far as I'm concerned, you should be six feet under."

"You plan on taking care of that anytime soon?"

Jared opened his car door, and warm air rushed in as he got out. *Great.* Exactly what he needed. Brock followed out the passenger door. Whatever they would hash out, be it scheduling his payback or coming to an understanding, he didn't want to do it while standing. His legs hurt too bad.

"How we gonna do this, Jared?"

Jared spun and glared. "I should kill you."

"You've never been all talk, man. What's it going to be?"

With his fists clenched at his sides, Boss Man stepped to him. Chest to chest, they squared off. "I don't trust you."

"You shouldn't." Brock had never seen Jared stumble for what to do before.

Fury ripped across Boss Man's face. "I blew up your house."

What? "In place of what, killing me? Or that just to piss Sarah off so she doesn't have a home to go to after my funeral?"

A tiny smile cracked across Jared's face, but he shut it down with a foul glare. "We've been through years' worth of fighting side by side. And shit, I get the do-anything-to-save-your-girl concept."

The explanation for not executing Brock was about as close to a heart-to-heart as Jared would ever have. *My turn... what to say?* "I knew that you'd get to Sugar before anyone hurt her."

"Maybe you did. Maybe you didn't. That's not the point."

"So what is?"

"Titan. Our team. We're fuckin' family."

The reminder was a twisting knife to his gut. "Yup."

"But the house is a goner. That pretty truck of yours is too."

Such a Boss Man thing to do. Brock almost had to laugh.

Jared blew out through clenched teeth. "I needed to destroy something before I came here to scoop your ass up. Otherwise, maybe you would be dead right now. We aren't even. But we're as good as we're going to get at the moment." He growled. "And I need to thank you. You took the kill shot when I couldn't. For everything you screwed up on our last job, you also saved Sugar's life. Thanks."

Brock stood there, nothing to say. He never expected a thank you and wasn't sure he deserved one.

Jared marched toward the driver's door. "What's your problem? Get in the damn Rover."

He pivoted toward Boss Man. "This has been too simple. I mean, hell, man. I deserve worse."

"Well, get in the car. You'll have Sugar to deal with soon enough. She might not want you dead, but she does want five minutes with you. Alone. Death might be the easier option."

THIRTEEN

Calming her nerves, Sarah sipped her strawberry daiquiri while she and Sugar lounged by the pool. They'd put Bethany on a private jet back to her parents earlier, and it was time to unwind. If she could. But Jared had been gone for hours, and anxiety whispered awful thoughts to her.

Sugar plopped on the lounge chair next to her. "Always wanted to come here on vacation. Think we'll stay a few days." She narrowed her gaze at Sarah chewing the end of her straw. "Relax. They'll be fine. Both getting Brock out safely and working out their man crap."

"Maybe." She gnawed on the straw, took another long sip, and gnawed again. She needed to focus on something entirely different. The men would be fine. Working herself up wouldn't help a thing. "I think I'm going to find a job when I get home. Assuming Brock and I work out some details. No idea what he's going to do, but the girls and I aren't hiding anymore. They'll be in school, I'll be… doing something."

Sugar swallowed a huge gulp of her drink. "Yeah, about that. When you say *home*, it might be more figuratively than literally."

Sarah raised her eyebrows. "What's that mean?"

"Jared blew your house up. Big-time. Huge explosion. Ka-blam-ie."

"*What?*" She choked over her daiquiri. "He did *what?*"

"Sorry, chickadee. Boys will be boys and all."

Sarah started laughing. She couldn't stop. Her life was insane. Their existence was completely ridiculous.

Sugar frowned. "It's not really funny. I'm being serious. I tried to stop him but—"

Sarah put her hand out to shush Sugar. Tears streamed down her face. *It is that funny.*

"Sarah, are you okay? Don't crack up on me." Sugar put her drink down and clapped in Sarah's face. "Oh my God, I'm going to have to call Mia or something. Snap out of it."

She tried for a breath, but it turned into a snort. Then she started laughing all over again. It felt great.

Sugar covered her mouth. A bright lipstick-covered smile peeked out from behind her fingers. Then she laughed too. They laughed and drank and laughed some more.

Finally, Sarah shook her head. "I hated that house. I didn't want to go back there anyway. Starting new will be awesome. New house. New school. Hell, new marriage."

A pool boy brought them fresh drinks.

"But you're keeping Brock, right?" Sugar slurped the last of her drink and grabbed the new one.

"Yeah, but we're going to try to keep things a little more exciting." She wagged her brows.

Sugar clapped again. "Good for you."

"Now I just need a job and—"

She sat upright. Excitement bubbled onto her face. "Come work at GUNS!"

"What?" Sarah laughed, shaking her head. "Me at your gun range? My last visit there was traumatic, and I barely know a pistol from a rifle. You don't want me."

"I'm serious. I need a little help around the office. Some marketing stuff. I want to play with logos, branding. Things are changing a little since I left the ATF, and, ya know, it'd be fun."

Fun? "I can..." Other than Brock, she hadn't let anyone know she could draw and design. "I can do artistic stuff."

Sugar bounced in her seat. "Perfect. Decision made. You can work with me."

"What the heck?" The decision was liberating. "All right. I'll do it."

Sugar sat back in her lounger. "The boys are gonna love this. And look, here they come."

Sarah glanced over her shoulder. Brock limped in clean, baggy pants next to Jared. They rounded the corner of the pool, and she giggled watching just as many people jump out of their way as stared at them. They looked like action figures crashing a beach party.

Sugar bounced up. "J-dawg."

"Baby cakes." He hooked an arm around her. "Didn't know you packed a bikini."

"Yup, did that while you were running around, placing C4 charges in their kitchen."

He glared at her. "Sorry about that, Sarah."

She shrugged. "I'm good."

Brock's jaw dropped. "You're good?"

She nodded. "Gives us an excuse to move closer to GUNS. I work there now."

"What?" Both men were in unison.

Sugar laughed. Sarah did too. *Talk about shocking two guys who thought nothing fazed 'em.* As if on cue, the pool boy walked up and offered pink frozen drinks. Jared took his. Brock waved his away.

For the first time, Sarah was completely relaxed. She kicked back on her lounger, grabbed her daiquiri, and closed her eyes. *All would be okay.*

EPILOGUE

Three months later

This was Sarah's second trip to Saint Lucia. Last time, she'd been nervous, unsure, and a little crazy. *Maybe a lot crazy. Who knew?* But this time, she knew what she wanted, and it was her man to come back from his shopping excursion. She checked out the clock again. *Brock should be back any minute.*

Tonight they would renew their wedding vows. Their kids were with Grandma now. A slew of Titan and GUNS friends were on the island too. But right now, Brock and Sarah had the afternoon alone and were revisiting their shopping list. They'd intentionally skipped ropes and ice cream on their at-home to-do list, waiting until they came back there. Seemed corny at first, but at this moment, it seemed hot.

The door lock unlocked, and her stomach jumped. Sarah sat on the bed, legs tucked under her, with nothing on but a grin. "Took you long enough."

"Turns out, I had to go to two different stores." He held up a container of vanilla ice cream and a bundle of rope. "And you, angel, get to pick which one we play with first."

"Ice cream." She giggled and bounced on her knees. "And rope."

His eyes were trained on her chest then drifted downward. "Whatever you say."

Brock tossed the rope onto the bed and ripped off his shirt. His erection pressed evidently into his pants, and she reached for him, stroking him.

"On your stomach."

"Stomach?"

He raised his brows. "Do it."

She flipped over but kept her gaze trained on him. He smiled and used a tactical knife to unbind the rope then cut the rope into strips. Methodically, he laid them at the foot of the bed. Excitement buzzed through her body as she stared at the four-poster bed. Her heart beat faster with each second she waited for him to pay attention to her.

Brock climbed onto the bed, straddling her naked legs, and walked his hands up her thighs, her bottom, her back. His palms flattened against her shoulder blades, and their heat burned clear into her heart.

Arousal pounded inside her, waiting for his next move. Both her arms were tucked by her side, and he took her left arm, slowly moving it to reach in front of her, then did the same with her right.

He leaned forward to kiss her neck. She shivered from anticipation and would kill to have more contact. But that was also part of the fun. His hands snaked up her biceps then forearms. One hand grabbed both her wrists while the other wrapped a line of rope around and around, securing her hands together.

"Such a beautiful body," he growled, still hovering over her.

Brock shifted off of her, opening the ice cream container and unbuckling his pants. The two sounds stole her breath. Wetness dampened between her legs, and a throbbing need for his touch made her almost delirious.

Sarah turned her head to face him.

"Close your eyes, angel." A devilish smile flashed. "Or don't."

A second later, he had pulled a silk pillowcase off a pillow and tied it over her eyes. His rough hands drifted down her back, stopping on the swell of her bottom. Strong fingers flexed and massaged. He bent over her, his tongue tracing an imaginary pattern on her skin. His teeth scraped along her side. Her skin reacted, so sensitive and aching for whatever he would do next.

A frozen surprise touched her calf. A heavy spoon ladled with ice cream dragged up the back of her leg. Melting streams slid on her skin. Larger scoops stayed in place, slowly melting ice cream drops on either side of her calves and thighs.

The sensations tickled down her leg, making her toes flutter and fan. A shiver ran up her spine. Icy coldness heated her mind. Then his tongue licked a liquid tendril off her calf. Strong, hard hands bent her leg at the knee, bringing her ankle to his mouth. Brock kissed, licked, and lapped at ice cream as it slid down to the backs of her knees.

"So sweet." He bit and nibbled when his mouth came to a torturous stop. Languidly, he placed her ankle back on the bed. His tongue swirled behind her knees.

Shivers erupted on her legs. A moan escaped her lips. His name fell from her mouth, aroused and husky, and her head twisted on the bed.

He smiled against her skin. His tongue snaked up the back of her thigh, cleaning away the ice cream, replacing the sticky cold with his mind-bending hotness. His branding kisses caressed over her cheek then skipped to the other side.

"Please, Brock." She turned her head again, hoping her urgency would be conveyed. But he trailed his lips down her thigh, slowly, as the ice cream melted on her body.

"Feels good, doesn't it?" And again, he repeated the ankle lift. The gentle sucks, the insane laps, clearing away the coldness and nuzzling into the sweet spot behind her knee. His lips were chilly but his tongue so warm. "Tastes even better."

I had no idea that could feel so… amazing.

"There's a new spot." Cold lips dragged.

Her breathing was erratic. "Uh-huh."

One hand smoothed the back of her legs, nudging her open, then swept across her wetness. "You like it."

She nodded. "A lot."

"Good to know, angel."

Somehow, having her wrists tied together, her eyes blindfolded while his fingers explored her, made *angel* sound sexier than ever before. She pictured herself sprawled inches from the massive wood headboard. The carved bedposts feet away. Her body clenched, wondering how and when Brock would make use of the ropes he had cut. He wouldn't be delicate with her. Not now. Not when she'd be crying out his name.

"No more teasing. I was wrong." Broken breaths barely allowed for complete thoughts. "I just need you."

His fingers drifted over her bottom, damp from her juices. He feathered his hands up, moving his muscled body between her legs. "The buildup's too much? My sweet angel needs relief?"

"Yes." She pulsed, needing his tantalizing touch again. But he tormented her instead and laid his heavy shaft along the ridge of her rear, stroking up and down. She widened her legs, searching for friction against her clit, but the position she wanted seemed painfully out of reach. Completely impossible.

"Want some help?" His voice was guttural. Antagonizing.

"Yes." She nodded, wanting to see and loving that she couldn't. "Touch me. Tease me."

His chest pressed against her back while his lips toyed with her earlobe. Brock's hand slid down her sides, cupping her hipbones. "You sure about that?"

"Yes." Her hands jerked at the ties. "Brock, please."

The pads of his fingers smoothed forward. He toyed in the damp curls, curving and caressing until he found her clit. The tease was so needed, so unexpected. It stole her breath, revived her need. She felt swollen and ready.

He sucked down the back of her neck. His weight crushed her to the bed until he slid to the side. One quick move and she was flipped over. Arms still overhead and bound, legs free, and knees bent. He had to give her more.

The end of a rope tickled her stomach. Electricity sprouted across her skin. *Oh, how'd I forget so fast about the other ties?* Her sensitive flesh went on red alert, and Brock scratched the cut end from her collarbone, down the valley between her breasts, over her clit, then made fast work of securing a ligature around her ankle. Straightening her leg, he tied her ankle to a bedpost. The other leg didn't receive the same finesse. It was bound and tied in a second.

She couldn't see him, but she could sense him. Feel his gaze and knew it was centered on her, open to him.

"Beautiful." He walked along the side of the bed, flipping additional ropes in his hand. Each slap made her shiver. He leaned over to kiss her lips then tied her already-bound wrists directly above her to the headboard.

Arms together, legs spread, and blindfolded. Her body couldn't wait for whatever came next.

A small spoonful of ice cream landed on her nipple. His tongue followed its path as it melted and slid to her breastbone. His fingers tweaked her other nipple as he busied his mouth. With each pinch and tug, her body jerked. Her pussy clenched. "I have to touch you."

She wanted to. Needed to. Her fingers would latch onto him, drawing him closer. Ending this torture.

"You will. But I'm not done yet."

Ice cream dropped onto her belly button. His lips encircled it, his tongue lashing into the delve of her stomach, while his fingers brought her to the brink of agony. One hand palmed her breast, massaging and tugging. The other hand curved over her mound, two fingers finally pressing in.

"Yes." It was all she could manage. "More."

Incoherent thoughts. One-word pleas. Her legs struggled against their bindings. The rope scratched into her flesh, sending lightning strikes screaming up her legs. His fingers began to fuck her, in and out, roughly pushing her toward a climax she was dying for.

Sarah's back arched. His hands worked in tandem. Stronger. Harsher. Everything she wanted. And then his cold lips kissed her clitoris, and she lost her mind. Her body thrashed, and she cried for her husband.

"Come for me." It was a command. Its rumbles pulsed against her intimate flesh. He had no intention of letting her fall away from this. His eagerness, his determination made her love him all the more.

Her climax sealed her eyes shut behind the blindfold. Fireworks exploded, rocketing, radiating to every tied-up limb of her body. Her legs quaked. Her fingers interlaced, locking into a struggling, surviving clutch.

Brock maneuvered over her and lifted the blindfold from her eyes. Sarah blinked. His smoky eyes and chiseled face hung above her as she focused. He stared, deep and meaningful, touching her soul, until she could semi-regulate her breath. Still tied but able to see, she picked her head up, her lips meeting his, and she kissed him until his arms wrapped under her, hugging her to him.

His erection pushed into her, slowly, inching in. "I love you, angel."

His lips swept over hers. His tongue stroked hers. His arms remained around her, hugging while he stroked her from the inside out, owning her. Driving her mad with love and comfort and devotion.

She could come again just from the sound of his voice, from knowing the profound commitment Brock had made to her, to their family and future. He still hugged her, still stroked her, but it was faster and deeper. His breath raced with hers. They were sticky, sweaty, and in sync. Her climax rolled through, and his followed. Brock moaned and bit onto her shoulder, groaning and spearing her deep.

"I love you too." Her superhero. Her husband. Their new life together. She loved it all. In a few hours from that moment, they'd be showered and dressed, standing before their family and friends to recommit to their promise of love. But in his arms, knowing that he'd given her *more* than she'd initially known she wanted, Sarah vowed to always take the risk, to be his Gamble. Brock and Sarah Gamble. Together forever, always searching for their *more.*

THE END

CHASED

ONE

Asher McIntyre left the keys in the front door of his Georgetown row house and stared at the note taped to the mirror right inside the door. His heart thudded, more angry than apprehensive. He didn't need to read the printed paper to know who it was from.

He turned to his alarm system panel. It blinked disengaged and ready to arm. He had turned the pricey piece of garbage on that morning. His note-leaving friend had officially upgraded himself from creepy to criminal.

Asher couldn't stand in his doorway all night and growl at a piece of paper. It was safer to turn around, walk to a coffee shop, and call for investigators to sweep his townhouse, just like they'd done with his car and office days ago. But his head pounded after hours of congressional hearings, constituent meetings, and lobbyist meet-and-greets. He wasn't in the mood to smile pleasantly if he accidently bumped into a reporter or blogger. His soured attitude would be speculated about and end up as political fodder. Every misstep would be analyzed for the next six weeks, until Election Day.

Asher cracked his neck, snagged his keys, and took a step inside. His shoe echoed on the hardwood floor, and he swiped the note off the mirror.

Dear Congressman McIntyre,
Still watching you. Still waiting. Time to right your wrong. Let's meet soon.
Best wishes,
Maxwell

Asher shouldn't have touched it. Could have read the note's nonsense while it remained taped to his mirror, but he didn't want the stupid thing mocking him until the investigators came. He shrugged off his jacket, loosened his tie, and pulled his smartphone out of his pocket. *Is all this worth it?*

He scrolled through his contacts and found the special agent who had handled his previous notes and hit send.

It rang once. "This is Murphy."

Asher scowled. "A new note was waiting for me today."

"Give me one second." The agent excused himself from someone on the other end of the line. "On your car again?"

"Nope. Inside my townhouse, taped to a mirror." He paced his living room. An invasion of his privacy wasn't anything new, but Asher had no idea what Maxwell was after.

"Son of a bitch. Don't touch—"

"Too late." Asher tugged off his tie, tossed it on the couch, and headed for the wet bar.

He ignored the *People* magazine he'd thrown there the night before. It wasn't his type of magazine, but his campaign consultant had mailed it to him. The headline stared up from the bar. A fifty most beautiful people list. Five bucks said his name was on that list somewhere, and for the next few weeks, he would have invitation after invitation to events that he didn't care about from women who wanted to appear with him like he was their fashion accessory. Every time a list came out, the same charade unfolded, and every time, it gave him a headache.

"Are you kidding me? You know better than to touch evidence."

That made Asher chuckle. Murphy was formal because he was supposed to be. But they were about the same age and had the same get-the-job-done disposition. By the time they found Maxwell, he and Murphy would probably be buds.

Asher poured a glass of scotch and shrugged. "Sorry, man. Anger got the best of me. I would've stood on my front porch, giving the finger to anyone interested, but then I'd have to deal with that picture on the front page of the *Washington Post.* One nuisance at a time."

"I'll head your way with a couple guys. We'll be discreet."

Asher swirled the drink in his hand and walked into the kitchen. "Thanks, man—"

Another note was centered in the middle of his stainless steel refrigerator. His Georgetown home was where he crashed, not really his home. That was in New York. Asher had no personal items in DC, certainly not a picture magnet of his sister and her best friend. They were younger by five years and had spent the past week in Disney World for a wedding reception. The picture on the fridge showed them posing in front of Epcot Center.

His hands shook, and his jaw cemented shut. A harsh breath flared through his nostrils. "Murphy, send the whole goddamn FBI."

"Care to explain?"

"There's a recent picture of my sister and her best friend, along with another damn note from Maxwell. *Aren't they cute?*"

•••

Jenny Chase tugged her carry-on bag out of the overhead compartment. The flight from Florida to DC had been bumpy, and she wanted off the plane. In the seat beside her, Molly was unfazed and casually powering on her phone and listing off where they should grab dinner before they headed home to their apartment in Eastern Market.

As long as Jenny could grab a cocktail, she didn't care where they ended up. Molly's phone buzzed. Once. Twice. Then kept going.

"Jeez, popular much?" Jenny watched her best friend's phone continue to vibrate.

Molly laughed. "Just Ash. I'm sure whatever it is, it's super important, and I need to know super right away." She slipped the phone into her purse. "Let's have pizza delivered instead of going out."

Just Ash. Just the man that starred in every fantasy that Jenny had ever had since she could remember fantasizing about a guy. Of course, he was probably the star of many women's dirty imaginations. He was Hollywood handsome and Washington powerful. That combination did wicked things to a woman's fantasies.

Jenny silently chanted, "It's only Ash." *Only Ash*...That was how she needed to think about him because both Molly and Jenny had given up that anything would develop.

Shoot, even now her cheeks felt warm. What thirty-year-old woman couldn't kick a high school crush? How many nights over the years had Jenny confided to Molly that she loved her brother? Too many, all starting back in high school when she'd circled his name in hearts. Even when Ash had flirted with her in college, the sparks had never panned out to anything more than heated glances and breathless moments.

Jenny tried to act nonchalant. "Maybe you should see what he wants. That sounded like a lot of phone calls."

"Text messages too," Molly added. "He hates to be ignored. Not everyone hops to his attention when he wants something. Drives him crazy."

Kind of like he drives me crazy. Jenny shuffled through her purse without reason. Pathetic, really, but every time he came around or called, she became a mess.

Over the years, Asher had become rich and famous. Incredibly important. She wasn't in the same ballpark as him with her hodgepodge of jobs. Nothing that would constitute a career. Jenny helped her sister, Sugar, with the gun shop and range she owned. But mostly, she honed her craft. She was an actress. A few good parts here and there. A few commercials. A couple of cable pilots that had never taken off. But live performances were what made Jenny's heart flutter and pound.

Much like Asher McIntyre did. She laughed and ignored Molly's sideways glance. Her mind had come back full circle to him. No one stacked up to him because, like it or not, she'd been in love with him since she'd met him. Just like no other type of acting stacked up to the roar of an applauding crowd on opening night.

Whatever. When she needed an Asher fix, all she had to do was read a newspaper or check a tabloid. He was all over it, pretty girl hanging on his arm.

Molly nudged her. "Jenny? Pizza? You okay with delivery?"

"As long as we stop and grab a bottle of wine." They moved into the plane's aisle and trudged into National airport. The crazy flight was the topping of a crazy week. Jenny couldn't comprehend that Sugar was married now. Her sister was the wildest, toughest girl she knew, and Sugar had basically eloped in Vegas, adopted a kid, then celebrated her wedding reception at Disney World. Sugar always knew what she wanted and got it. *Me? Not so much. Part-time gun-range assistant, full-time wannabe acting star.* At least it kept the bills paid and offered a super lax schedule.

"Wine. Good deal." Molly nodded.

They rounded the corner from the long hallway into the airport waiting area. Six men in black suits waited, watching each passenger. Their stances and their looks screamed that they were packing heat.

Jenny knew those types all too well. Hard to ignore them when Molly worked with the high society of the political world, and when Ash was *the* Asher McIntyre, Mr. Rising Star Politician, the congressman who was soon to be the senator to New York State. Hell, probably soon to be president, give him enough time. And even if he didn't carry that title, he had any number of Most Eligible, Most Handsome, Most Beautiful crowns that had been printed for the whole world to see the smile that about made Jenny pass out from hormonal over-exposure.

Congressman today. Senator in a little more than a month. President...whenever he wanted. His career was just another reason why nothing would materialize into a relationship. Ash was world famous; everyone hung on his every word. And she was clinging to an acting career where no one seemed interested in watching her say anything on stage. *Stop that! Big audition in a couple days. They'll love me.*

The leader of the suits brigade stepped in front of Molly. "Ms. McIntyre, Ms. Chase, come with us."

Molly turned to her, rolling her eyes and cracking a smile. "Guess I shouldn't have stolen the bathrobe, huh?"

"Should've checked your text messages and voice mail," Jenny whispered back.

No matter how many times law enforcement escorted Molly somewhere for work or inspected their apartment after the McIntyre family had another threat, men with badges made her nervous.

Other passengers streamed around as the obvious men encircled them. "Congressman McIntyre has asked that you come with us."

"Of course he has." Molly was used to the protective detail routine. She never looked concerned. "And you are?"

"Special Agent Murphy—"

"FBI?"

The man nodded.

"Give me a second to talk to Ash." Her best friend fished her phone out of her purse, hit a button, and had a fast conversation that ended with her mouthing, "Fine. We'll go with you."

Jenny picked up her carry-on bag and let the men whisk them to baggage claim. "Least we don't have to take the metro."

Why not have an armed caravan take them home? It was the perfect ending to a crazy week and crazy flight.

TWO

Asher stared out his sister's living room window. The FBI entourage pulled up and double-parked. He'd had the apartment swept, and nothing out of the ordinary had turned up.

Molly jumped out of the black SUV.

He kept watch. Waiting. *Waiting...* And there Jenny was, back turned toward him. He wanted to look away. Needed to, in fact, but didn't. His hand rubbed over an ache in his chest. He'd been forcing his thoughts away from Jenny Chase for the better part of knowing her. Little good that had done.

When he found Maxwell, Asher was liable to give up his entire political career and tear him apart limb by limb for threatening either woman.

Molly ignored the fanfare of an FBI escort, grabbing her bags and trouncing toward the front door. But Jenny stood outside the SUV, not shutting her door. Apprehension hung on her shoulders, and still she wouldn't turn around.

Look at me.

Then she did. They locked eyes, and he swallowed hard as her gaze fell to the street. *Such a gorgeous girl.* He knew the deep caramel bronze that painted her eyes, could see her dark hair even when his eyes were closed. Years ago, he had sworn off any woman who would be a distraction from his career. Maybe that made him self-centered, but really, he considered himself determined. Why be in a real relationship if he couldn't commit to anyone but himself? Man, that made him sound like a jackass. But it was the truth, and he didn't want to hurt his sister's best friend. Hell, he didn't want to hurt Jenny.

Even if the chance for something to materialize out of their spark had existed once, he had missed the chance, and an unspoken rule had formed between them. *Don't cross the line.*

The door flew open, pulling his attention away from Jenny. Molly stormed inside, tossing her bag and a purse. "Want to explain the security detail in more depth than 'there was a threat'?"

"In a second."

Jenny walked in but didn't speak. She avoided eye contact, and Asher craved all their flirty fun that rarely happened anymore. Maybe she'd grown tired of their game. If anything, he was more entranced with Jenny now that her interest in him was waning. It wasn't in him to lose. *She's not a game, dick. Get yourself in check.*

Three agents followed Jenny, reminding him that this wasn't a social call. Shit, he didn't care. He needed to hear her sultry voice. "Jenny."

"Asher." Her glossy lips teased him, making his name purr.

God, was she a sight. Every part of his body had readied for her to walk in. Even the hair at the nape of his neck continued to tingle.

"Haven't seen you around." That was what he came up with? He sounded like a dull politician, and that was how she saw him anymore, anyway.

She shrugged.

He'd blown her off too many times. *For all your smarts, you're a moron, McIntyre.* In Jenny's eyes, he was nothing more than a suit who gave speeches. His eyes fell to a pile of magazines on their coffee table. The same damn *People* magazine was top of the pile. *Great.* So he was either a dull politician, or, according to tabloid crap, he was hopping from one actress's bed to the next.

Molly tilted her head toward the waiting agents. "What's with the welcoming committee?"

He gave an apologetic smile to the agents. "How about you girls sit down? I need to chat with Agent Murphy."

She shook her head. "Nope. Jenny and I planned to order a pizza, throw on our PJs, and drink a bottle of wine. None of that can happen until you've explained whatever the incident is this time and everyone leaves."

Murphy cleared his throat and tilted his head down the hall. This wasn't going well. "Give me a minute."

Asher followed him to the kitchen.

"We can leave a man here if you'd like, Congressman. Other than that, there's not much to do other than keep an eye out."

Asher's gut tumbled. He liked proactive measures and was sure that the investigators working on the notes were chasing all possible leads. But still, one man outside? It was better than nothing, but he wasn't thrilled and couldn't call in a federal favor to babysit them. "If that's what you recommend, we'll take it. Thanks."

He returned to the living room as Murphy pulled his men and left.

"Here's the deal. Someone left me a couple threatening notes. Nothing out of the ordinary. But today, one of the notes included a picture of you both at Disney World."

Molly's face paled, and Jenny's jaw dropped. He wanted to comfort them both for the same reason in very different ways.

"No one's going to hurt you. They're just trying to get my attention." *And they fucking have it.* "This is precautionary."

"What's precautionary?" Molly asked.

"There's an agent outside. He'll stay there and keep an eye out." Asher wasn't ever unsure of his moves, but the one he decided that minute made him both unsettled and uncertain. He plowed forward. "And I'm staying on your couch tonight until I figure out what the best move is."

What did Jenny sleep in? His throat constricted. Silk draped over her curves would be nothing short of spectacular. The woman was his walking, talking dream. Shit, this spend-the-night-on-the-couch idea had major flaws. What good would he be if all he could think of was *don't touch* instead of *watch out*?

"The couch?" Molly's shaky voice brought him back to reality.

Jenny didn't move. Didn't respond. Her hands clung to the couch cushion as if the idea of him sleeping under the same roof was dangerous. *And it was.*

He took a long breath and pulled out his phone. "Pizza and wine is on me. We'll figure out what to do so I don't have to sleep on the couch another night."

"I'm leaving tomorrow." Molly rubbed her hands on her thighs. "Work trip for two weeks." She jumped up and paced. "We should have a bottle of wine in the kitchen. I'll grab it and some glasses."

If he did spend a second night, it would be just him and Jenny? His mind raced. The idea was too much to comprehend. He had spent years avoiding her temptation, and now he could barely stay away. Why? Because he'd put her in danger?

Molly started down the hall. "I can't believe someone followed us in Disney World."

He watched his sister then turned back to Jenny. "We have to talk tonight. Hang tight."

He followed Molly, and she spun. Her lip quaked. "I hate this stuff, Ash. I need a minute to wrap my head around it, then I'll be fine. Okay?"

She clung to the door jamb in the kitchen. She liked her privacy, and every time he dropped a bomb on her, she needed a few minutes on her own, then his kid sister was back. "Got it."

If any of the tabloid magazines had a clue that he was getting booted back and forth by the two women he was trying to take care of, they'd have a field day. Two different ladies. Two different, very raw feelings bit at his mind. Protecting them both was crucial. He wanted to go all patriarchal on Molly and all alpha possessive over Jenny.

Rubbing palms into his eyes, Asher tried to think of anything besides Jenny's pouty, pink lips.

He rounded the corner blind and slammed into soft, luscious curves. Instinct took over. He caught Jenny and pivoted. She found her balance, back against the wall. His left hand landed high above her head. His right caged around her waist. They stood the closest they'd ever been. Decadent warmth radiated from her body. Whoa, she smelled sweet. Delicious and mouthwatering. Butterscotch and vanilla.

He swallowed away an immediate urge to breathe her in and remembered his quickly fading rule *don't cross the line.* "Where were you going?"

Her long eyelashes fluttered. "It'd be better if I stayed somewhere else tonight. Let you two do the sibling thing. Ya know, a McIntyre family slumber party."

"Is that what you want to do?"

Her cheeks blushed, and hell if he knew why he'd asked that question. What he did know was the *don't cross the line* rule abdicated his rule book. Now that he'd broken their unspoken proximity barrier, he couldn't get close enough to her.

"It'd be safer if you stayed here."

"I'm heading to New York for an audition tomorrow." Her eyes bounced over his shoulder, and what he wouldn't do to have her lay those beauties back on him.

"Look at me."

She bit her bottom glossed lip. "No."

"Why not?"

Her eyes flashed to him, searing him straight to his groin. "Not everyone listens to you all the time, Mr. Congressman."

"I don't care if you listen or not, but I do care if you ignore me."

"What difference does that make? You've been ignoring me for years. Now if you don't mind, back up."

They stared, silent. He savored the electric charge that pulled them closer and leaned over. His lips hovered near her earlobe. "I'm tired of pretending."

Jenny pushed his chest and ducked under his arm. *"What?"*

The pounding in his chest reverberated into his throat. Two hot marks burned him where she'd pushed her balled fists. The tips of his fingers prickled to touch her cheeks, her hair, her curves.

Asher narrowed his focus on her but leaned against the wall.

She stepped backwards until the back of her legs met the couch, then she dropped onto it.

Molly walked into the room, much calmer and holding a half glass of wine in one hand, an opened bottle and two glasses by their stems in the other. She pivoted a look from Jenny to him and back. "Everything okay?"

"Your brother has lost his mind." Jenny pulled a blanket over her and burrowed into the couch.

He shook his head. "Actually, I think I just made my mind up."

•••

The living room turned into a sauna, and heat crawled up Jenny's neck. Her heart pounded into overdrive. She couldn't swallow past the knot in her throat, couldn't respond with any witty comeback that would make their banter nothing more than an innocent flirtation. Asher wasn't acting innocent, and she had no idea what he was doing.

Done pretending and made up his mind? Her mind spun around his words. *What?*

He was messing with her. He had to be. Nothing else made sense. Flirt and walk away. That was how their at-an-arm's-distance relationship existed, even if she wanted more. Even if she'd die for him to hold her against the wall like that again.

She shivered at the memory, even while self-doubt and self-preservation had her snuggled onto the couch with a blanket as a protective barrier. If she let him have his way with her, she would be irreparably broken and just another notch in his bedpost.

Asher picked a book off a nearby shelf, paged through it without looking, and tossed it onto the coffee table. It covered a magazine Jenny knew had a photo of him with a real actress.

Molly laughed for the first time since they'd learned about the threats. "You two kill me."

He crossed his arms over his chest. His eyes twinkled as if he were letting Jenny in on a secret, but then he turned toward the kitchen. "I'll call for the pizza, then have to make a couple phone calls."

"No prob. Take your time." Molly offered her a wine glass.

She unburied her arm to grasp the stem and held it steady while Molly filled it.

"More, please." Jenny wiggled her glass. "Or just give me the bottle and a straw."

Molly rolled her eyes toward the kitchen where Asher could be heard ordering pizza. "What just happened between you two?"

Jenny shrugged. "Same thing that always happens. He flirts, walks away, and I'm left looking silly with a sad crush."

"That's not what happened. I can tell that much." Molly topped off Jenny's glass and sat on the other end of the couch. "What'd he make up his mind about?"

She took a long sip of the wine, not bothering to enjoy it. "No idea."

"With the way you're draining that wine glass, I'd say that's a lie."

Jenny tilted her head and knew she blushed. "Maybe a small one."

"The wine is helping?"

"A little." She swallowed another massive drink. "A lot. I don't know."

"Better watch out, that wine's going to hit you fast on an empty stomach." Molly picked up the remote and skimmed through their DVR.

Nothing looked good. Jenny could still feel Asher's arms around her, and the scent of his cologne lingered on her shirt. Cable reruns weren't going to be any form of distracting entertainment. One minute turned into five minutes, then fifteen, and Jenny had no idea what had been on the television. All she could picture was his arms around her.

"Molls," she whispered like he might be hanging around the corner and not ordering pizza or discussing national security or whatever he was doing on the phone in their kitchen. "He said he's 'done pretending.' What does that mean?"

Molly's smile went as wide as her eyes. "What *does* that mean?"

"I don't know." Jenny chewed on the inside of her mouth. "He had me up against the wall."

"He *what*? The wall?" Molly's jaw hung open, and she inspected the wall like there might be evidence of the encounter. "No way."

"I'm being serious." Jenny rubbed her temples. "Why did he do that? I'm totally reading into that, right?"

"Shoot, Jenny. What's there to read into? A man presses you against the wall and says he's done pretending? For years, I've been saying it's only a matter of time. He's all book smart and politically savvy, but the guy is obtuse when it comes to finding a decent woman." Molly kicked her leg off the couch and knocked the book Asher had placed on the table to the floor. The latest *People* magazine was front and center. "Case in point, that couldn't possibly have been a serious thing."

They both knew that there was a picture of Asher with an A-list actress who'd fumbled through an E! interview, unable to recall how many states the US had. She and Molly had replayed that a hundred times.

Asher walked in. "Pizza's ordered. Should be here in a hot minute." He glanced at the book on the floor and the magazine they stared at.

He arched an eyebrow and gave half a smile. "Always up to no good." He tossed the book back over the cover and winked. "You doing okay over there, Jenny?"

"Stop messing with me, Ash."

"And miss a night with my two favorite ladies? Never." Asher dropped in the middle of the couch. His arms spanned behind both of them as he leaned back. "What are we watching?"

Molly topped off her glass of wine. "Actually, I have a headache." The doorbell rang. "That was fast. I'll get it, grab a slice and my glass, and head to bed. Nothing better for a headache than pizza and vino. You paid for this already, right, Ash?"

"Yup." He didn't shift to the empty side of the couch.

Holy shit. Jenny wanted to hug and strangle Molly. *Don't leave me alone with him. I'm not sure of my next move.*

"Night." A laidback Asher leaned forward, letting his hand drag over her shoulders, then grabbed the empty wine glass. He filled it to an appropriate level, unlike Jenny's monster glasses. "Feel better, Molls."

Molly brought the pizza to the coffee table, grabbed a slice without a plate, and left the box on the table.

This isn't at all awkward. And by not at all, all Jenny could think of was yes, this was obvious and awkward. The big, pink elephant in the room had donned a tutu and was dancing with sparklers in hand.

She gulped her wine. "Molly doesn't really have a headache."

What? Shut up, Jenny! Her nerves made the room shrink. She couldn't take a stabilizing breath and had no idea what uncensored line would fall from her lips next.

Asher shut off the television, turned, and raked a penetrating gaze over her while sipping his wine. Her nipples grew tight, and she shivered to her toes. The room was too quiet.

Finally, he swirled his glass and set it down. "I know she doesn't have a headache."

"You know?"

His expressive eyes narrowed. "You know what else I know?"

No. I don't. She shook her head. *And I'm not sure I want to know.* Her handling of his newfound focus left her quivering like a waif of a woman. Actually, drinking like a wino-sailor. The push-pull of their flirtation had never allowed for him to make a move. It was their unspoken rule, and apparently, she'd grown more than confident he'd never make a move. Tonight, she was unprepared.

"Guess, sweetheart."

Sweetheart? She shook her head again. *No way am I guessing anything.*

He smiled in that trusting, all-knowing way he had about him. "Here's what I know. First, someone threatened you girls. I'd walk away from everything I have to make sure justice is done. But second"—he took her wine glass out of her hand—"I needed to find you, Jenny. I need to put a stop to the one lie between us that has been as consistent as it has been irrational."

"That's the line of a politician." Taking a deep breath was out of the question. The wine made her head swim. *He* made her head spin. She tried again to fill her lungs and felt them refuse. There wasn't enough oxygen in her ever-shrinking living room. "You could mean anything."

"But I don't." He took a piece of hair hanging over her eye and tucked it behind her ear. Her pulse screamed in her neck, but his focused stare never wavered. "You know what I'm talking about. You've always known. Now it's your turn: What do you want?"

Her eyelashes fluttered; her stomach dropped. His voice was always low, but its vibrations washed over her, making her throb.

"I want..." *You.* That was the answer. It had always been the answer up until the opportunity presented itself. But she didn't trust her feelings or his motivation. "Not to be confused."

He shifted closer, evaporating their distance. His broad palms covered her cheeks, and his thumbs stroked slowly. Her bottom lip drifted open, and her eyelids sank. The quietest sigh fell from her mouth, and she hated how easy she was to manipulate.

"You are gorgeous." His tone was deep and hungry, and he was close enough for her to register the rich aroma of his faded cologne. "And it shouldn't have taken me this long to tell you that."

Asher brushed his lips over hers. Like the intense roll of a summer storm, crackling lightning and thundering pulses ran their course, uncontrolled and unstoppable.

"Ash…" Her lips tickled against his, and her mind drew blank, focusing on the sparks that spread from her lips into the softest of kisses.

His fingers feathered into her hair, and she opened her mouth to him. He tasted like red wine, sweet and savory, and each velvet stroke of his tongue wicked away her hesitation. She struggled to stay in the moment, wanting to remember every amazing second, but the indulgent and delicate kiss was fading. Years of taunts and teases had lined up, urging their bodies together.

Jenny leaned into his embrace. He dropped a hand from her hair and wrapped it around her back, pulling her close to his chest, into his lap. Exactly where she wanted to be.

He ate at her mouth, lust pouring between them. He was all-powerful, all-consuming. He groaned against their lip lock. "God, Jenny."

Her legs straddled his thighs, and she rocked her hips, flexing over him. His hand still buried in her hair knotted and tugged, exposing her neck. His teeth dragged over her bottom lip and scraped down her neck.

"Yes." His teeth rasped again, and she arched into his strong embrace. "Please, Ash. Please."

Please what? It didn't matter, whatever he'd give her, she would give back. Jenny wouldn't hide from him.

He suckled down to her collarbone. Harsh and surprising. The more he kissed, the more she needed. Pent-up frustration multiplied. Wild want pulsed between her legs. She was wet. He was erect. They still had their clothes on, and nothing about this first kiss said it was ending anytime soon.

"God, sweetheart, nothing better than you."

Red-hot in his arms, Jenny grasped at him, wrapping her arms around his impossibly broad shoulders. He picked her up and swept her down. Her back was on the couch, and he loomed over her then dropped down with a mind-bending kiss, pressing his weight between her thighs. One leg stayed pinned between him and the back of the couch, the other snaked up his strong, lean muscles.

She opened her eyes, skipping her hands into his hair. He leaned to the side and tore at her shirt, pushing it up her stomach, over her bra, and locked his mouth around her nipple.

"I love that." Intense pleasure-pain roared through her as he plucked and sucked. "I love..." *You.* She always had. But that wasn't for him to know. No reason to ruin this.

He pulled the other bra cup down and covered her breast with his palm. His massaging fingers were better than she'd imagined, and as he rolled his tongue over one tip and his thumb and forefinger over the other, she couldn't feel anything other than the ecstasy rolling from his touch, moving lower, lower, lower, all the way to her craving canal.

"Keep moaning like that, and we'll never make it into your bed." His light-colored eyes had darkened. Their shocking intensity made him look possessive, carnal—

A loud rap on the door froze Jenny into place with her hands gripping his shirt. They stopped. Their uneven breaths and heaving chests mirrored one another, and his head dropped, placing one languid kiss over the breast he'd been deeply sucking.

Asher pulled her shirt down. "Change in shifts. New agent. They'll need to check in with me."

He sat up as another rap echoed on the door and ran a hand over his face. Jenny pulled her legs back, flushed and dizzy, then scooted back on the couch, staring at him. *What to say?*

A third knock banged through the apartment, and Molly walked down the hall. "Jeez, isn't anyone going to—" She did a double take, and Jenny knew they were so busted. "Never mind. I got it."

Asher stood up. "No. Hang on. You're not answering the door when there's a lunatic out there." He walked to the front door, looked out the peephole, and answered.

Molly mouthed, "Oh my God," and pointed at her brother then Jenny.

Cheeks flaming from arousal and awareness, she shrugged, pulling the blanket over her. She mouthed back, "Go away."

Asher walked in with the agent and made introductions. The congressman was back; whoever the man on the couch was had been shelved. They finished small talk, and the agent moved to his post. Asher shut and locked the door, turned, eyeing both her and a giggling Molly. *Very mature, Molls.*

The hot and heavy moment was *so* gone, and they'd been *so* obvious, she had to laugh too. Even Asher-the-Congressman chuckled, and Jenny pulled the blanket over her head. "Go away, Molly."

Molly stopped giggling and whistled as she walked out of the living room. "Scandalous."

Still under the blanket, she heard Asher walk across the room and felt the cushion dip when he sat down. "You okay under there?"

"I feel like I'm fifteen and just got caught making out with the captain of the football team."

"Nope, just your best friend's older brother. Can't wait for the Molly McIntyre inquisition." He tugged the blanket off her head. "You're gorgeous and cute. Not a bad mix." Then he tossed the blanket back on her head. "Feel free to come out if you're hungry for cold pizza."

Well, she was hungry and would have to come out eventually anyway. She let the blanket fall.

"That was fast." He turned the lamp off and the television on, snagged her arm, and pulled her against him. Just like that, he was relaxed again and holding her.

She didn't get it. Not that she wanted to complain, but why now? "Ash?"

He took a bite of pizza. "So what's your audition for?"

She reached over for a piece of pizza, grabbed a copy of the script that'd been buried under the pile of magazines, and handed it to him. "Third callback, and I'm hoping third time's a charm."

"*Tassels and Tangos.*" He read the cover and paged through the bound script one-handed while his other arm draped over her. His muscles shifted suddenly from kicked back to killer. "Who's Maxwell?"

"An acting coach I met at the last audition. Said he had some insight into what the director wanted, but I got a weird feeling. That's his number in case I change my mind."

Asher's face hardened. He tucked her in, took her script, and walked to the door. Jenny leaned over to try and listen but didn't pick up any of the conversation he had with the agent. After a minute, Asher returned, sans script.

"What's that all about?"

He shook his head. "Nothing. Probably coincidence."

Icy dread curled down her spine. "Asher. Tell me."

"All the notes have been signed by Maxwell."

THREE

Asher wrapped his arms around Jenny and held on tight. Her run-in with a man named Maxwell wasn't a coincidence, and Asher wouldn't take someone fucking around with his family or his woman.

Jenny sighed as she watched *The Late Show* in his arms. This wasn't how he'd thought his day would end. No way she could've guessed it either. She had to be exhausted. Flight from Florida, glass or two of wine, and he'd basically jumped her out of nowhere. Add the spike of arousal and then the dread of a stalker—the girl needed to pass out.

As much as he wanted to take her to her room and strip her down, it wasn't going to happen tonight. "You falling asleep, sweetheart?"

She yawned. "Nope."

"Right." Besides, if he put her in bed, then he could follow up with Murphy, make arrangements for someone to talk to Jenny first thing in the morning. Maxwell contacting Jenny was a huge a break in the investigation. But Maxwell's blatant move had been dangerous. Asher wanted to pace the room like a caged tiger, ready to rip flesh from bone given the chance to attack. Jenny didn't need to see him worked up.

He scooped her up. "Off to bed."

She blinked, innocent and uncertain. "You joining me?"

"Not tonight."

Her face fell. Why had he stayed away from her this long? And how badly had he hurt her over the years? *Damn, McIntyre.*

"It's not that I don't want to. I have to work a little, and you have *Tassels and Tangos* tomorrow. Gotta get your beauty sleep."

He walked down the hall with her pressed against his shirt. He'd denied himself this simple luxury for years. Holding her couldn't compare to any other woman. And kissing her... wow. Not equivalent either. She tasted like honey and smelled like vanilla. A kiss from anyone else was akin to licking cardboard. Lifeless and unnecessary.

After opening her door, he laid her on the bed. "You okay?"

She shrugged, grabbed a huge T-shirt from the foot of her bed, and changed. Her modesty was charming, but he had stolen a glance at her lace bra and thong and loved knowing what was under her cotton nightshirt. Somehow that peep show was even better than what he'd imagined with his earlier thoughts of silk pajamas.

"Not sure I can sleep." Her voice was worried.

"Forget about Maxwell." Saying the man's name made Asher's blood boil.

Jenny crawled under the covers. "Trying."

A vortex of emotion swirled in his mind. Like. Lust. Longing. He traced her chin with the back of two fingers. "You are as soft as you look."

"Stay with me tonight."

He should walk out. Stay away. Board up her door and call in for reinforcements. But one bat of her eyelashes, and he was done. Kicking off his shoes, he crawled next to her and brought her to his chest. *Butterscotch and vanilla.* He was in deep. Asher kissed the top of her head. "Sweet dreams."

•••

New York vibed well with Jenny. Even in dirty Penn Station with people cruising past, cops standing around, and pickpockets manning the walls. She rode the escalator up with a duffel bag slung over her back. *This is my break. I will get this part, and I won't worry about Maxwell.*

An icy chill ran down her spine. Jenny peered over her shoulder incessantly and tracked for any face that rang remotely familiar. She was terrible with faces, even after Agent Murphy had questioned her bright and early that morning. *After I woke up next to Asher.*

Both men had pestered her with questions, but all she could remember was a short and stocky man who acted like he had something to prove. He had cut her off and talked down to her. When she had met Maxwell, she'd thought his hard sell was the source of her discomfort. But thinking back on it, maybe her instinct had flared because her Maxwell and Asher's Maxwell were one and the same. That jerk had been trying too hard to get her alone.

Forget about Maxwell. She mentally rehearsed her favorite lines from *Tassels and Tangos* until her phone rang. She fished it out of her purse—*Asher*—and her stomach flipped. Maybe they were really happening. She touched the screen to answer. "Hi."

"Hey, sweetheart. How was your trip?"

"Easy enough." She shivered. Asher's chiseled face had been stuck in her head. She replayed every kiss and touch from the night before. "We were on time."

"Good." He took a long breath. "Did I mention waking up next to you made my day? We should do that again soon."

"Oh." She couldn't breathe. Couldn't swallow. "No. You didn't."

"Ouch, but you're not signing up to do it again?" He laughed.

"No, wait. Of course." She rolled her eyes, snapping out of her fog. "Don't tease me. This is all a little surreal to me."

"Why?"

She stood at the crosswalk next to a newspaper stand. Facing her was a slew of New York daily rags. More than half of them had his picture above the fold. "Hold on." She snapped a picture and texted it to him. "Because I'm a nobody, and you're a little like a modern-day Prince Charming. Check your text messages." She waited until he came back to the phone. "See what I mean?"

"Ignore it. I do."

"Ignoring." *Yeah, right.*

"So, I made arrangements for a protective detail for Molly while she traveled. And you too."

She crossed the sidewalk with a gaggle of people, eyeing each one for Maxwell. "What's that mean?"

"A friend is former FBI, does private security and undercover work. I think he'd fit in, and he can work with you until the Maxwell situation is wrapped."

"You're assuming I'll get the part?"

"Of course I am."

The audition building was straight ahead, and adrenaline shot through her system. "That's confident of you."

"Sweetheart, you should assume the same thing. Anyway, his name is Ricky, and he'll play your acting or choreography coach. Something like that. I couldn't figure out what he was talking about, but he knows theatre, and he'll find you. He's hard to explain. Never what he seems, so just go with it."

"You didn't need to do that, Ash."

"Of course I did. I would've done it even if last night didn't happen the way it did."

"All right. I'm here. Talk to you later." *Because we chat on the phone now. That's your new normal. Own it.*

She looked up at the towering building. This was the third time she would walk through the doors, and Jenny was ready to give the audition of her life. The script had been permanently embedded in her mind. It was sexy. Fun. The costumes were outrageous. Bright. Feathery. Full of sequins. The part was hers—it just had to be—and promised to be a big debut.

Jenny pushed through the spinning doors, took a deep breath, and was tapped on the shoulder.

"Took you long enough. I'm Richard." His name fluttered into the air, full of pizzazz. "You can call me Ricky. All my friends do." He spun around the lobby. "I love this location. Love! Great audition rooms. Good energy."

What? Ricky was nothing like she'd expected of Asher's former FBI friend. Not at all. "You're Asher's friend? Were with the FBI?"

"Takes all kinds." He took her fingers in his hand and held them like they were promenading in a royal court. They walked toward the front desk to check in with security. "Sixteenth floor." Ricky pointed at Jenny, and they handed over the IDs for a quick inspection. "Third callback. She's a surefire winner."

"Good luck, miss." The security guard handed back their licenses, and they were allowed access to the elevators.

They rode in silence to the sixteenth floor. Somewhere near the seventh floor, Ricky donned his invisible security person hat. "If anyone asks who I am, I'm Ricky, your coach. If something bugs you, doesn't feel right, or if Maxwell walks in and you remember his ugly mug, you just wave your pretty little hand at me, and I'll take it from there."

She blinked. "You'll take it from there? How?"

"What do you mean, *how?*" He rolled his eyes but did a little karate chop. "Should I get out my guns and thump my chest? Maybe do a push-up contest? Would that make you feel better? Though I'd much rather get an iced mocha latte and talk about your posture."

My posture? What's wrong with my posture? She was sure Ricky hated her all of a sudden. *So much for making friends with the guy.* And she could see why Asher had struggled to explain her protective detail.

"Don't gawk, Jenny. Not a great look on you, and you're super cute. Don't do yourself any injustices." He sized her up. "I can see why Congressman McIntyre is so…vested in you." He paused again then nodded. "You need a massage. And maybe a snack. A wheatgrass smoothie. Does wonders for the mood, you know?"

Actually, maybe they would be friends. She'd be friends with anyone who suggested a massage, no matter the reason. She checked her phone. Ten minutes until her audition time. "No time, but afterwards, absolutely. Wish me luck."

Ricky took her hand and swung it. "Break a leg."

•••

Nothing had turned up from the phone number Maxwell had given Jenny. Failure made Asher's skin crawl, and even though Ricky was with her, he cleared his schedule and hopped on the train to New York City.

In the span of one night, Jenny had gone from being someone he refused to touch to the woman he refused to stay away from.

The high-speed train wasn't getting him there fast enough, and despite all the campaign calls and emails he could do, he let his mind wander. *Tassels and Tangos.* What was that about anyway?

His campaign consultant called again. It had to be the tenth call in a row. He growled, not wanting to take it, but did. "Yeah, McIntyre here."

"You're in New York?"

"Almost."

"What about your fundraiser tonight with—"

"I canceled that."

"I know you canceled it. Any particular reason why, or should I worry you've lost your mind six weeks out from Election Day?"

Asher laughed. "You're the second person in as many days to tell me I've lost my mind."

"Not funny."

"I'll make it up. I swear."

"This is why you pay me the big bucks. Already worked that out for you. All you have to do is make an appearance at some swanky dinner tonight at some fancy New York City restaurant. Try to smile at the big donor's very pretty daughter a few times, and we're good."

He pinched the bridge of his nose. "*We* aren't anything. I'm done with the arm candy."

"I didn't say you were her date tonight. I'm saying that her big-money daddy wants you two to meet, and he was hosting the fund-raiser in DC that you've decided to skip. So there isn't much to discuss here, Congressman. Make the guy happy."

Asher growled to himself. Election Day loomed. He couldn't afford rookie mistakes, and pissing off a major donor was amateur. "Fine. Done."

He hung up the phone. It rang again. But it was Jenny.

"Asher?"

The giant pressure leaning on his chest melted at the sound of his name rolling off her tongue. "Hey, sweetheart."

"I got the part," she nearly screamed into the phone. "They gave it to me."

"You earned it."

"I earned it." She made an excited noise, and he was pretty sure that Ricky was jumping up and down with her.

Only Ricky could pull a move like this one. Such a chameleon. One of the toughest brutes Asher had ever met. That man could morph into any role he chose.

"Guess what?"

She giggled at something in the background. "What? Tell me."

"I'm on my way to see you."

"Really?"

The excitement in her voice was so genuine, it reminded him of how she was the opposite of every manufactured meeting, date, interview that he'd dealt with lately. "Really."

"Oh, but they're starting right away with costume and publicity shots. I have a whole schedule of things to do this afternoon."

"I have a way of being invited to places I don't need to be. No one really tells me no. So, I'll be there. Don't worry." The perks of being the up-and-coming senator—it should all go according to plan.

Forty minutes later, he'd covered a few blocks in the Fashion District, where her rehearsals were. Ricky had sent him the details, and Asher hauled to see her. His suit looked out of place, and his tie strangled his neck. At a red light, he stood next to a few hipsters and a man pushing a cart of dresses.

Dodging a wayward taxi inching through the horde of bodies, Asher breathed in the city and let excitement charge his blood. Energy revitalized him after the hours on the high-speed Amtrak train.

He found the building, was waved through security, hit the sixteenth floor, and pushed past a gaggle of models who all looked like Barbies. He stepped over a red-head kid in pigtails lying on the floor, reading a commercial script for apple juice.

This place is a madhouse. He rounded the corner toward the room number Ricky had texted him, pushed the door open, and—

Holy hell…

Dry mouthed, Asher slammed to a halt, nearly stumbling over his own feet. Jenny was busy talking to the seamstress at her knees, who sewed something shiny onto something that glittered. Under the glaring lights, Jenny sparkled.

But the glittering getup—the sky-high heels, corset, and fringe—had nothing on her flat stomach, perked breasts, and legs that every model in the hallway would commit homicide for. Asher stared, drinking her in, too shocked to move or even wave hello.

A man carrying a clipboard swaggered around Jenny, inspecting her. He pushed his glasses into his hair, put his knuckles to his chin, and studied. Asher contained a primal roar. The bastard might not live through the day. He fisted his hands into his pants pockets and needed to calm the urge to rip the guy's eyeballs out.

Ricky bounced over, a feathery mess slung over his shoulder. "Costumes are going well. This is the last one to get fitted—"

"Who's that?" Asher growled.

"Talking to Jenny? That's the director, Colton. Cole for short."

"Well, Cole's too close to her." Asher took a step forward, fists still in pockets, rage bubbling as the man adjusted a strap on Jenny's leg.

With a flip of the feathers, Ricky tapped Asher on the chest. "Mr. Congressman, get it together."

Asher stifled another urge to maim and growled again instead. "Richard—"

"Maybe you need a smoothie too. She's in such a better mood since I gave her a snack."

He eyed his buddy. "I'm impressed, by the way. Have me fooled."

"Whatever." He flicked his hands out with the feather rope then drew it back at Asher's scowl. "What, you don't like my boa?"

Jenny looked over, finally noticing him, and laughed. She did look in a good mood, much better than the last time he'd seen her when she'd been gnawing on her nails over Maxwell.

He nodded at her half-naked, jewel-costumed body. Jenny had stunned his thoughts silent.

"What do you think?" She gave a spin, ignoring the seamstress trying to keep up with her.

He pinched his eyes closed. What did he think? Thinking about her was his problem. He could ditch big money's daughter, find a hotel room, and they wouldn't leave for a week.

"I need to speak with Jenny." Asher stepped toward her. "Alone."

Cole took a step back from her, eyebrows bunched, but stopped and walked forward, extending his hand. "Congressman McIntyre, so nice to meet you."

Asher moved across the worn, wooden floor and completed the obligatory hello. The seamstress smiled and waved as she passed. Even Ricky stepped out, which surprised Asher.

Mirrors surrounded him on three sides. Floor-to-ceiling windows served as the fourth wall.

"How do I look?" Her fingers knitted together like she was suddenly nervous under his attention. "I'm going for hot, but, ya know… So?"

"You want hot? Pretty?" Were there even words for how she looked? "How about you try every man's lifelong fantasy? You're making Victoria's Secret angels look like knobby-kneed bums."

She laughed, and her already-red cheeks flamed. "Thanks."

"My lifelong fantasy."

Teetering on breakneck high heels, she stopped fidgeting and looked up from under the sexy veil of her eyelashes. "Really?"

Asher stepped to her. He dropped his hand to her flat stomach between the corset top and the sequin bottom, and his finger traced softly. Her skin was velvet. They were suspended in the moment, Asher holding Jenny to him with the strength of a gaze.

Her chest rose and fell, mirroring his tempo. Jenny sucked her bottom lip, nailing him with textbook bedroom eyes. Her palm found his, smoothing it from her hip, over her bare stomach, and stopped on the corset. She leaned against him, pushed onto her toes, and pressed her lips against his ear. Warm breath caressed him, and his mind spun.

A knock on the door, and Cole popped his head back in. "You guys good? Photographer's here for her promo pieces."

He dropped his finger but ignored the director. "I need to get you out of here."

The room filled.

"Asher," Ricky sang to him. "I got you a smoothie. Wheatgrass with strawberries. It'll help your mood, whatever's wrong with you."

She shook her head. "I have to work. And then there's a happy hour I have to go to. We're celebrating... me, I guess."

He stepped back, drawing a fresh breath and hoping for some perspective. "I have a dinner thing to go to too." Ricky stood next to them with a green smoothie. It looked disgusting.

"Try it." Jenny smiled. "Pretty good, actually."

He shook his head. "No, thanks."

"Take it anyway." Ricky pushed the cup into his hand and turned to Jenny. "I'd say the congressman looks horny, but that'd cross the line, wouldn't it?" Ricky winked at Jenny and walked away.

She covered her mouth, shocked and laughing. "Oh my God. How well do you two know each other again?"

"You could call us old poker buddies." *I'm going to kill him.* "All right. You do your thing; I'll hit this dinner and find you afterwards." He turned and walked away. Each step felt heavier than the last. Jenny was permanently seared into his retinas. But he had to take one last look. He turned and stared over his shoulder. "See if you can bring some of that outfit home tonight. I'll put it to good use."

FOUR

Agent Murphy's name appeared on his phone, and it was the perfect excuse to bail on the boring dinner party. Asher had done his piece. He'd said hello to the right people, discussed all the issues and impending legislation that dinner guests had asked about, and even thrown out a few insider-only campaign details that the dinner guests would love and he needed leaked. *Like the new poll numbers that had him holding a solid lead over his opponent.*

He answered right before the call would hit voice mail. "Hey, Murphy. Tell me you have good news."

"I have good news."

"Really?"

"Well, it's news. A lead. After combing through your old constituent mail, we found several letters from M. H. Bowie. Recognize the name?"

"No. But we get thousands of letters, e-mails, phone calls. I don't handle them myself."

"This guy showed up at least once in your office last year, but we don't think you ever saw him. Met with your deputy chief of staff after harassing a couple interns."

"M.H. Bowie is Maxwell?"

"Bowie's first name is Maxwell. He's the fifth Maxwell Bowie in his family. All military, all the way back to the revolutionary war. We're talking steep family history."

"How does that relate to the notes?"

"New York seized his home under the claim of eminent domain. A highway is under construction, and Maxwell's family home—they call it the Bowie Estate—is where an exit ramp is planned."

Asher nodded. "I know about the so-called Bowie Estate. They've applied and have been denied for historic and national landmark designations. The Bowies have zip in terms of documentation."

"Exactly. And Maxwell the Fifth was dishonorably charged from the Army after a few incidents. His psych evaluations fit with the profile of someone trying to redeem himself in the eyes of his family."

"So Maxwell Bowie is our guy? Got a picture of the dick?"

"Not one hundred percent positive, but he's the best we've got. We'll get his picture and file e-mailed to you. Now for the bad news. He's also off the radar. Don't know where the bastard is. Here's the deal, Congressman—"

"Asher."

"Yes, sir. If it is him, he's not your typical politically driven stalker. He's had some mid-level specialty training. Enough to make him dangerous."

"Just terrific." Asher blew out harshly as he hailed a cab. "I've hired a protective detail for Molly and Jenny."

"Well, actually, sir—"

"Asher." A yellow taxi pulled over, and he hopped in and gave the intersection for the happy hour. He looked at his watch. *Five minutes, tops.*

"Yes, sir. But you are my concern."

"I'll be fine. As a matter of fact, I'd welcome a sit-down with Maxwell the Fifth. I have a few things to explain to him."

"I can appreciate that, sir—"

"Seriously, Murphy. My name is Asher. Call me Asher."

Murphy laughed. "Not as easy as it sounds."

Asher could almost hear the *sir* and shook his head. "Find Maxwell. We'll stay in contact. After all this is over, we'll go grab a couple beers and shoot some hoops. See if you're sirring me then." He hung up the phone before Murphy could offer another *yes, sir.*

The taxi pulled over, and he shoved the cash through the slot in the safety glass. Less than five minutes, not bad. The bar was on the corner, and he walked in.

Jenny stood out in the crowd. Her back was turned with her dark hair piled up, but he could pick that woman out anywhere. Her laughter carried from the bar across the loud room, and she tossed her head back. Unaware of him, and Asher was content to watch.

Graceful neck. Sexy, strong shoulders. She reached back to toy with loose strands, and the move punched him in the stomach. Those arms needed to wrap around him, and his fingers would be in her hair, again and soon.

He walked toward her, ignoring the occasional nod of recognition from folks downing their after-work cocktails. Ricky sat at a nearby table, watching Jenny, studying everyone in the room, and making small talk.

Two men flanked Jenny. Both could back off, but Asher wouldn't concern himself with them. For all he cared, there was only one other person in the room. That gorgeous girl who'd teased him over the years and had become a focal point the second he'd grasped what she meant to him. Maybe he had one thing to thank Maxwell for, and it was that realization.

One last step, then Asher pressed against her back, her ass, and nuzzled his cheek behind her ear.

"Guess you couldn't go walking around in your costume, huh?" He let his lips tickle the edge of her ear and inhaled her light perfume. She smelled delicious. "What are the chances you brought that thing home?"

Jenny stayed caged to the bar and tilted her head. "One of the perks of my new gig is a furnished, temporary apartment. Rumor has it the closest isn't empty."

He closed his arms tighter, and warmth penetrated his suit jacket and shirt sleeves. "Yesterday, I had you pinned against a wall. Tonight, against a bar. Hoping you like that as much as I do."

Her breaths stilted and hitched. He was close enough to feel the irregular cadence. Close enough that he could savor it, enjoying the prickles that swept across the nape of his neck and shot down his spine.

Slowly, Jenny spun in his arms. She focused on his tie, then her hands found his coat lapel. The delicate touch glanced off the fabric, sliding down its edge until her hands fell to her sides. She raised her chin, and the heat in her eyes nearly made him kiss her right in the middle of the bar, in front of the world. That would make tabloid gossip rags before they even left. She didn't need that. Nobody did.

"Your dinner went fast."

"I couldn't stay away. Let's get out of here."

She looked away at a few people he recognized from the audition room earlier. "I can't just walk out."

"You're right." It was selfish to steal her from her celebration. Didn't keep him from hovering close enough to kiss her lips. "I'll—"

One of the men next to her stepped closer. "Jenny, this guy bothering you?"

"No. I'm not." Ash's chest rumbled when he spoke.

Another guy elbowed the man who'd interrupted. "Oh, man. That's—"

A split second later, the flash of a camera phone caught him broadside.

Shit. He ducked his head. Ricky walked over, and Asher heard a brief exchange that resulted in the picture being deleted.

Her eyes were wide. "Maybe we should go."

"Don't worry about it." Ash grabbed her hand. "Tonight's your night to celebrate. Ignore that; next round is on me."

He tucked her close and flagged down the bartender.

Another flash of a camera.

She spun toward the camera. "Do you mind?"

"Ignore it," he whispered. "Just you and your buddies here tonight. Forget everyone else."

"That *was* one of my so-called buddies." Her brow furrowed, and she mumbled, "Bitch."

"Don't react." He knew how hard it was to ignore. "They'll get bored, and the pics won't sell if there's nothing interesting."

She burrowed into his arm. "All right."

Another snap of a camera. *Damn it.*

One of the men raised his glass. "To Jenny's new part and the free publicity." Several people clinked glasses and offered happy-hour cheers. A couple more clicks of cell phone cameras sounded. Asher could hear Ricky in the background working his way through the crowd, trying to let her have a semblance of privacy. Maybe Asher should have thought this through before he'd shown up.

She smirked at the man who offered the cheers then turned to Asher. "It's not like that. You're not free publicity."

"I know." Too bad this had New York's trashy newspaper coverage written all over it. "I messed your night up."

"Screw them. I want to bail." She ducked her head. "Let's go."

His arm went around her shoulder as they turned to leave. Asher nodded to Ricky, who he knew would do his best to clean up the pictures. Jenny leaned against him as they pushed through the mess of barstools and bodies. Her sweet scent teased him. Asher dropped his chin to the top of her head. "I wasn't trying to cause a scene, sweetheart."

"I know." She nodded as they broke through the front door. He kept her close, walking them down the street, going who knew where. Just away. Her heels clacked over the sidewalk, catching on the cracks and toeing over the grates, until they rounded a long city block and stopped.

He couldn't stay away and had to taste her kiss. She backed against a building's brick façade. His shirt touched hers. The swell of her breasts pressed to his chest. He cupped her jaw, sliding his fingers into her thick hair.

"Congratulations, by the way." He kissed her, and her welcoming response seared into his soul.

"I earned it." Jenny knotted her hands into his starched button-down, sighing against his mouth.

The confidence in her words turned him on. Hours earlier, she'd been unsure if she would get the part, then she did, and she had realized that talent was on her side. Just yesterday, she'd wavered into their kiss, uncertain of him. But today, she teased him in a glittered costume and with her wicked tongue.

Asher nibbled her lip, tugging until he felt her smile. She slipped her tongue over his. The velvety slash caressed straight to his straining erection.

Her arms snaked up his chest, locked around his neck. Flexing her hips into his, Jenny rubbed into his hold, and he was consumed and possessed. Everything about her made him hot. Made him lose control. His senses were inflamed, and her touch, her kiss branded her to him.

She belonged to him. In his arms. In his bed. *She's all mine.*

Asher pulled her into another kiss. Tongues clashed, lips molded. Together, they were ravenous. He dropped his hands and cupped her ass, picking her up, letting her long legs wrap around him. The effect was catastrophic. The V of her legs shifting against his shaft made him insane.

The honk of a horn and an angry driver yelling out a car window broke his thoughts. His eyes were forced open. They were a few hundred feet from a main street. Even this side street would have the occasional taxi passing through. Fondling her against the wall was the wrong move. They were too public. Too many people could walk by, snap a picture, and sell it to a gossip rag. It'd embarrass her. It'd be a headache for him. But her legs squeezed, her eyes asked for his attention, and he couldn't stop.

Asher jerked his hips into her. A strangled purr fell from her lips, and he slanted his mouth over hers again.

Another honk of nearby traffic.

She staggered a breath. Her cheeks were flushed. Her lips had plumped from kissing until he could barely breathe.

"Don't forget, they gave me an apartment." She blinked, and the rapid-fire flutter made her seem too innocent. "It's not far from here. Haven't been there yet. There's a key waiting."

The color yellow caught in his periphery. Without putting her down, he spun and whistled. "Taxi."

•••

They were at Jenny's temporary home-away-from-home ten bucks later. Not the greatest building, but it was the perfect location: five blocks from the theatre and half a block from the practice studio.

"The bellman has my key," she said.

Asher was the picture of cool and collected, completely unfazed as he led her into the building and took the key from the bellman. The envelope was labeled #2306.

Compared to him, she was a mess. Her heart punched her breastbone. Her feminine parts were in overdrive—breasts aching for his touch, dampness teasing between her legs, and a wild curiosity piqued. If kissing Asher was better than she could fantasize about, what would he be like in bed?

In the taxi, he had stroked her arm and made small talk with the cabbie. She had focused on breathing. *Inhale, exhale. Don't pass out.*

Jenny leaned against the elevator wall as it slowly progressed to the twenty-third floor. Asher's hand covered hers. She watched him in the mirrored walls. A wicked smile danced on his face as he watched her back.

His eyes were intense. His sinewy jawline flexed. He personified dapper and daring, as if he'd walked off a GQ photo shoot. Perfect hair. Perfect suit. Perfect… *just perfect.*

A sparkle radiated from him. Every woman wanted to be on his arm. Every man wanted to be his buddy. It made him a good politician. That, and he *was* a good politician.

He was the real deal, through and through. As manly and in charge as they came, and he'd set his sights on her.

The elevator doors opened, and in one step, he had her under his arm again and walking toward her apartment. Toward a bed and every dream she'd hoped for since they'd first been introduced.

"Here we go." He jangled the key and slid her in front of him. She pressed against the cheap wood, and he slipped the key into the lock, unlocking it, but didn't turn the handle. "What's that look?"

I can do this. I can do anything. Just calm down.

Tingles exploded down her neck, shooting toward her navel. Asher drew back, narrowing his eyes.

"Jenny?"

"This is going to change everything." There. She'd said it. He could agree and walk away. Everything would go back to normal, where she pined after him, he glanced her way but kept moving.

"Hell, it wasn't the same after we kissed." Asher turned the handle, held her against his chest, and walked into her new apartment. "I haven't been the same because of you. I've loved it."

Good, because I love you.

Their eyes were locked, and she couldn't turn away. Asher led her from a matchbox-sized living room to the tiny but separate bedroom. She'd been warned that the place was semi-furnished and decorated to get "their star" into the spirit of the show. Boas draped over the door. Candles lined a dresser, and erotic books lay on the nightstand. The apartment had a *Tassels and Tangoes* quality. Sexy. Seductive. Sensual.

With all the command of his importance, Asher removed his suit jacket. The tie came off with a fling and landed over a chair that held yet another feather boa. He mesmerized her, emanating confidence and dominance. The vibes made her stronger, more ready to take what she wanted and give herself to him.

He worked his cuff links. Each deliberate motion was sharp. Provocative. If he handled her the way he did his clothes, then the man was in charge and did everything just right. Her sex throbbed in anticipation.

"Someone's taking your show very seriously." He nodded to the boa and loosened his collar.

"It's an acting method. Immerse yourself into the role. I play a burlesque dancer."

Excitement flickered across his expression. "Come here."

The order made her tremble. It was exhilarating, a sampling of what would come. She stepped to him and began to undo his shirt buttons.

Asher toed off his socks and shoes. "What do I get to play?"

"What do you want to play, Mr. Congressman?"

"No, you don't." He chortled and tugged her shirt over her head. "Enough of that."

She studied him, sliding his dress shirt off his shoulders. It fell to the ground. "It's like you don't want the title sometimes."

"What I want is you." He yanked off his cotton undershirt. "It's never been about the title or the attention."

Asher's smooth, tan chest towered over her. He loomed large, protective. Hungry. An extraordinary thrill made her heady. A man who epitomized power and prowess wanted her.

Jenny laid her palms on his stomach then sashayed her fingertips over his rippled abdominal muscles and traversed to his sides. "Then what has it been about?"

"I don't want to talk about work."

Her fingers mapped the path of his belt. Undoing the buckle, sliding the clasp from his pants, the expensive material dropped to his ankles and his thick shaft bulged behind boxer briefs.

She outlined his shaft with the slow slink of her fingers over the cotton. "Tell me anyway."

"This is coercion." His head rolled to the side. "My standard answer, I like helping the greater good."

"I'm sure that's true." She cupped him and stroked. "But tell me the real answer."

He inhaled as she glided over his length then caught her with the flash of his eyes. "I love the knowledge and control."

Asher continued to stare. Gripping him tighter, she ran her tongue along her bottom lip, and his eyes tracked the premeditated lick. "I think I'd love the control too. I like it now."

"Sweetheart, you're going to be pinned to that bed and screwed until you scream if you're not careful."

She watched his face and bent to his pec, lapping below his collarbone. "Promise?"

He smelled like soap and the faint hint of cologne. He tasted as solid and crisp as a fall day, and never could she have guessed that her tongue would savor him.

She sat on the bed and brought him directly in front of her, again sliding her hands down his sides. "Don't move, Asher."

Leaning over, Jenny forced a hot breath through the fabric of his boxer briefs, over the crown of his cock. Asher sucked in a quick gasp. She kissed the edge of his skin, dipping her tongue below the waist of his drawers. "I want to taste you."

He groaned. "Sweetheart."

Her palms slid down to his hips, smoothing over his well-developed thighs and taking with them his boxer briefs. He stepped out of them and stood on display for her. Naked and sculpted. Virile and potent.

His erection was thick, massive, and reaching for her. "Ash..."

Her hands ran up the backs of his thighs, smoothing over the solid muscles of his rear. She nuzzled her cheek against his length, mouth watering. She could almost taste the salty, savory strength. As she squeezed him, he swayed. She could do anything she wanted, and he would let her.

"This is what it feels like," she whispered.

"What?" his voice rasped.

"You're one of the most powerful men in the world." Two hands rocked him, up and down. "This is how you must feel."

His eyes pinched closed. "And how's that, sweetheart?"

"In control. Confident. So sure of myself I might explode."

The corners of his lips ticked into a smile. "You and me both."

"Here's to a night of fireworks." Her mouth enveloped the broad tip, and his cock speared into her mouth. A hint of salt, the musk of sex... All her senses were alive.

She stroked and suckled. His muscles contracted, his breath stuttered. Asher's hands knotted into her hair, guiding and demanding.

He murmured her name, and each thrust reached for her throat. He was more than she could handle, like drowning on an unexpected dream come true. Heat flourished inside her womb, and she met every growl and groan he offered. Every erotic sound, taste, and texture made her core beg for attention.

She kept one hand on him, but the other unbuttoned the top of her pants and slid to the top of her panties. How many times had she touched herself while thinking of him? Her fingers found dampness. She widened her knees and took him further in her mouth, moaning as she touched her clitoris.

His breath heaved. "Are you touching yourself?"

She nodded.

"Fuck, sweetheart."

God, she wanted to taste him. She looked up, pleading with her eyes to keep going.

He untangled his hand from her hair and unclasped the back of her bra. She slid it off but stayed in the moment. Her body was reeling. Passion burned through her veins. Her pussy wept for him. Her clit had swollen, pleasure rolling and building.

He stepped to the side, moving to the bed. She stayed with him, going on her knees as he sat down. Asher sheared her pants and panties down to her thighs. His palm caressed her rear then dipped between her legs. Two fingers teased her wetness, toying with her opening. The pleasure was almost too intense.

She kept her fingers on her nub, circling, and kept her mouth on his cock, sucking. His thighs flexed and strained. Watching him struggle and tighten, feeling him harden even more in her mouth drove Jenny to the brink of orgasmic heaven.

Her hand on him dropped to his sac. He gasped and penetrated her with his fingers, sliding them deep into her canal.

"Jenny," he moaned deep from his chest, and Asher erupted in her mouth.

With his fingers still inside her, his seed pulsing in her, Jenny flew over the edge. She sucked him deep, and her pussy spasmed. Her clit pulsed. Waves of aftershocks roared.

Asher eased from her and pulled her into his arms. "Gorgeous, sweetheart."

Both their hearts beat wildly from rapture. With her temple pressed against his sweat-dampened chest, she could hear the barely slowing *thump-thump-thump.* The tempo mirrored the rabid cadence of hers. "I…" *love you…* "needed that."

FIVE

Asher's ragged gasps surprised him, but the white lightning igniting his imagination didn't. Hell if he had known Jenny would be so bold. Her mouth had been intense. Cataclysmic. But her confident strokes to both of them? He shook his head and rubbed her naked back. *And this is just foreplay.*

Her sexy smile and pink cheeks made his chest feel tight. What was she doing to him? Twisting his world from orderly and measured to uncalculated but full of possibilities.

Taking a deep breath, he was refreshed. Reinvigorated. Years of stress gone with one pretty girl having her way with him. No woman before her had even neared the level of playing field that Jenny now owned.

Hunger burned in her features. Every flirt and temptation before this night had been a silly game. How many years had he missed out on mind-bending climaxes? Too many.

"I want you naked, sweetheart." His hands drifted over her plump breasts. "And I want to touch you. Suck you. Have my way until you can't handle any more."

Jenny shifted from his arms and grabbed a black boa off the headboard. She tossed it over her shoulders. "I can handle a lot. Don't make promises you can't keep."

He laughed. "Think you know that's never been my problem."

"How do you know when a politician lies?" She twirled the end of the boa. "His mouth's moving."

"Ha, ha. Aren't you funny?" He kissed her then reached for her foot and removed a black stiletto. He dropped it by his knee then did the same with the other. She reclined against a pillow, and her dark hair framed her. The boa feathers flittered, and she twirled each end, flicking her wrists until she dropped them over her chest.

Asher tugged her pants off and revealed a skimpy, satiny black thong. It was all that she wore. Well, that and the black boa draped carelessly over her breasts.

He slipped the high heels back on her feet and stared. "Unbelievable."

Jenny kicked one long, silky-smooth leg in the air, and he caught her ankle. Black heels, black boa, and black thong. Dark hair. Pouty, swollen lips. Rouged cheeks. Jenny was pinup girl material. Pretty and erotic as a boudoir picture.

"I've dreamt of you, sweetheart. But this..." He crawled next to her in bed, caressing up her thigh and over her stomach. "This is more than my mind gave me."

She laughed, supple and rich, and the sound cascaded to his groin.

"Funny how we've had the same dream." One side of the boa slid off her breast.

The luscious mound and the tight nipple spiked unconstrained desire into his system. He bent to the tip, curled his tongue around it, and listened as she sighed. Jenny's back arched. He teased, working her deeper into his mouth, sucking the sweet cherry of her breast.

She clutched an end of the boa, and her hands pushed into his hair. Tiny flashes of pain rushed through him when she pulled in time with his mouth. The torture made his cock jump.

Rasping and tugging with his teeth, Asher watched Jenny toss her head. The lovely little noises she purred couldn't have made him any harder. He abandoned her breast and elicited her protest.

"Don't you worry." Asher kissed his way down the slope of one and up to the other. "I'm not going anywhere."

He breathed over its erect tip, flicking his tongue and brushing with her lips. Her hums started again. Her hips gyrated, and her stilettoes slowly inched up the bed, until her legs were bent and the icepick heels were near her ass.

"I ache, Ash."

He petted over her thong. "For me?"

She nodded. "Yes."

"For release?" His fingers slipped under the satin.

"Uh-huh." Her eyes screwed shut. Black feathers swayed by her arms.

"I could watch you like this all day long."

"Don't." Jenny gasped. "I might die."

He skimmed his fingers along the slick folds. "Like silk. Bet you taste like honey."

Her head thrashed. "Don't tease me anymore. I *am* dying."

They both were. Asher circled his thumb around her clit and his tongue over her nipple. Jenny's moans turned into pleas. Her hips swayed and lifted, the spikes of her black heels digging into the bed.

"Sweetheart, I'm having too much fun to stop."

"But I don't want to come alone." Her mouth gaped, and her eyes pinched. "Be with me. Please, Asher."

What was his holdup? Nothing, other than wanting to watch her fall apart again. He rolled from the bed, found his wallet, and slid a condom on.

Jenny propped on her elbows, knees still bent. He snagged her thong off but kept her heels and boa in place. He'd never wanted a woman the way Jenny made him want.

Sweat dampened his temples, tickled a spot between his shoulder blades. He wanted until he hurt. Wanted so much, so hard, that he wasn't sure that fucking her would do anything but exasperate his need.

Asher covered her body with his. His shaft touched her center, making him shiver. Jenny laid her hands on his shoulders. Each half-moon of her fingernails bit into his flesh. The scrapes and scratches surprised him and felt awesome. He hoped they'd leave marks and flexed his hips, pressing smoothly into her wet heat and hoping she'd claw him again.

Her muscles clenched as he impaled her. "God, yes, Ash."

Hunger surged, and he was losing himself in her. His thighs spread hers, and he worked deeper and deeper, feeling her fall open for him. They hit a sinful rhythm, and his name fell from her lips again. It was pure music. Almost lyrical.

Desperation and a fierce, barbaric, primal appetite controlled his body. He kissed her. Hard. Licking and biting and absorbing her essence. Just as hard as she kissed him back. Their mouths dueled. He wrapped an arm around her neck, and her heels crawled up his thighs, locking over his backside. He drove into her, and she embraced it, demanding more.

Goddamn, he was going to come. The release burned close. It made him blind. Made him crazy. Made him so sure he could love—

"Asher," she screamed his name. Moaned again. Her head hung back. "I need—"

She shuddered and froze, tightening in his arms. Her legs clamped against his back, and Jenny bucked. Her pussy rode his shaft, pulsing and throbbing at the intense demand of her climax.

He gave up his barrier, everything he'd been holding back. His mind was frenzied. His lust unbridled.

"Sweetheart," tore from his lungs, burned into the air. He pumped through the torrid peak, shattering in her arms, and collapsed against her.

Jenny wrapped her arms around his neck, pulling him closer to her. Her clenching sweetness still convulsed, and he gasped for breath.

Asher pressed his lips to hers. Not a kiss. The lip press was nothing more than needing to be connected in every conceivable way. He could fall asleep like this. Holding his heaven.

They floated down together into silence. Finally, he could catch his breath, and the blood rushing in his ears slowed. She didn't stir even as the boa's feathers shimmied. Her eyes stayed shut, but he didn't think she was asleep. What was going through her mind? Hell, what was going through his?

SIX

The unfamiliar bed might have coaxed Asher awake, but the warm woman curled naked against him was like a shot of high-octane espresso. He gathered her into his arms. "Morning, sweetheart."

He wasn't one for morning-after chitchat. But it seemed his standard operating procedures had officially become a joke. Nothing he did or said to Jenny was his norm. Nothing inside his chest felt normal either. It was tight, but he felt… fulfilled. Odd since he'd been driving for that feeling with every career move and election. The answer had been in front of him the whole time.

"I'm not a morning person," Jenny mumbled and burrowed against his side.

He reached to the nightstand and checked his watch. Seven in the morning. *Getting a late start.*

When was the last time he had slept in? He couldn't recall. A campaign conference call was in thirty minutes, but that could be done from bed. Mostly he listened while his re-election team discussed the campaign stops, polling, and focus groups.

If something interested him, he would pipe up. But the logistics of campaign work numbed his mind. Let him do his day job, then he'd be happy. But that's not how elections were won. There were fundraisers to attend, commercials to shoot, messaging to try.

Just thinking about the call bored him, but he had to get up and figure out what he should do about clothes. *Didn't plan this very well,*

McIntyre. His suit and shirt were strewn across the room. Wrinkles weren't a good look for a man hounded and photographed on the campaign trail.

He grabbed his phone and touched the screen. Too many e-mails and text messages to count. *Shit.* He'd forgotten that Murphy was e-mailing over the Maxwell file. He clicked the e-mail open and downloaded the picture. No one he recognized. The file didn't share any new information either.

Asher looked at Jenny. She snoozed quietly. Looked so innocent, though last night had proved that wrong. He would've whistled if he didn't have to explain why. The woman's sizzle was almost too much. *Almost.* But he'd take it. He smiled. Yeah, he'd take it every minute of the day.

He scrolled through the rest of his e-mails. *Campaign team, more campaign team.* More scrolling. A lot of e-mails overnight. Then again, he hadn't checked his e-mail since he'd jumped off the train. There was an e-mail from Molly, subject line, "Heads up." Nope, not in the mood for bad news. It could wait. Scrolling through more e-mail, finally, *press clips.*

Typical headlines. News on his opponent. News on the poll numbers. Typical. Everything that would be addressed on the conference call—well, whoa. What was, "McIntyre and Mystery Brunette"? *Jenny.* Guess Ricky hadn't gotten all the pictures taken care of.

That was also what Molly had probably e-mailed him about. His sister was sure to have press clips and a Google Alert set up to track his name.

He clicked the link open and scanned. Nothing overly interesting. A cell phone-snapped picture and references to Jenny's attractiveness and reluctance to leave.

He bet the "reluctance to leave" line would be fodder for gossip blogs and that his campaign team would say things like they should jump in front of the problem. Maybe issue a statement that Asher McIntyre respected women. The reactions sometimes were worse than just explaining the truth. His girl didn't want to leave the party in her honor, but some people had been dicks and ruined the night for her. *Glad I made it better, though.*

He chuckled, taking it more in stride than he should, then leaned over and kissed her shoulder. "We've been ousted."

She shushed him and nuzzled into her pillow.

"There's a picture."

Jenny slowly propped up on elbows. Her eyes were sleepy and hair disheveled. All in all, a great look on her, minus the annoyed pinch of her brows. "Picture? From one of the cell phones?"

He handed the phone over.

"Oh, this is bad, isn't it? For you? Politics isn't my thing, but this isn't great, right?"

He shrugged. "Seen worse."

She scrolled down and back up again. "They make you sound like a caveman, yanking me out of a bar."

"They said you were hot." He took the phone and tossed it toward the end of the bed. "Can't fault them for the truth."

"God, if I'd just walked out, none of this—"

"You can't second-guess yourself, and you know that everything I do is tracked by the local news."

She rolled her eyes then tried to smooth her hair. "Yeah, the man who hits every eligible bachelor list in the United States is tracked by just the local news."

Shit. What was he thinking? This picture pinpointed exactly where Jenny was and that she meant more to him than just his little sister's best friend.

His phone rang, but he ignored it. A gut feeling said nothing good was on the other end of that call.

"Hey." Jenny rolled to face him. "You okay?"

The phone rang again. He rubbed his face. Everything he did was calculated, but last night was not, and the sudden realization of the repercussions made his stomach sink. He grabbed the phone. Caller ID showed FBI Agent Murphy. He accepted the call and closed his eyes.

Asher took a deep breath. "Think I have a problem."

Jenny's face fell, mumbling, "Guess not."

"Yeah, I'll say," Murphy grumbled. "You didn't mention that Jenny Chase was more than your little sister's best friend. That changes a few things."

"It's a recent development."

Murphy laughed. "Yeah, well, guess those things happen. You also didn't mention that Jenny Chase is the sister-in-law of Jared Westin."

Asher's mind stumbled, and he coughed. "Excuse me?"

"Guess you're having quite the morning, aren't you, Congressman?"

His mind reeled. Habit almost had him correcting Murphy to call him Asher, but the bigger concern was Jared Westin. "I'll call you back."

He hung up, dropped the phone, and rubbed his temples. "Sugar married Jared Westin?"

Jenny nodded. "Yeah. Why?"

His mind raced. Jared Westin ran Titan Group, and they were more than qualified to protect Jenny than half the FBI. Given Titan's leeway with the law and its connections with everyone from the president to the director of the CIA, it would've been beneficial to know. That, and Jared would want to know if there was a threat against Jenny. The man had a ruthless bastard streak to him, and Asher was sure not being filled in on threats to extended family didn't conjure up a good attitude.

He pinched his eyes shut. Actually, why hadn't Titan shown up unannounced for protective detail? Only one reason.

"You didn't mention the notes to Sugar?"

Jenny shook her head. "She's just back from her honeymoon. Why get her in a tizzy?"

His stomach churned. He was very good at his job. Titan was very good at theirs. Much better than any resource Asher could call up, and he was man enough to admit that. "Because you were threatened. Because I can't be with you twenty-four hours a day, and Titan can offer far more in terms of protection than I can sleeping on your couch."

"You didn't sleep on the couch last night." Her smile flirted with him as she played the innocent card. "Besides, I don't think that's what Titan does. They take out war lords and cartel kings or whatever."

"Trust me when I say no one really knows exactly what Titan does." He checked the time and was a minute late for the campaign call. "Forget what you think you know about them, and call your sister."

•••

Jenny groaned and stared at her phone. Calling Sugar was never the easiest ordeal. She was pushy, and once her mind was set on something, it didn't matter what Jenny said.

Working with Sugar at GUNS was fun. But telling her that a stalker had snapped a photo of Molly and Jenny at Disney World? Not fun.

Nor would the inquisition be when she told Sugar that after years of pining after Asher McIntyre, he'd spent the night in her bed. At least she could tell Sugar about the part in *Tassels and Tangos.* Jenny nodded. Sugar would love the performance for no other reason than costumes were going to be unbelievably outrageous.

Speaking of which... Jenny climbed out of bed and wrapped a sheet around her. It was too early to call anyone. *God, what time did Asher start working?* It wasn't even eight yet. She watched him pace in the living room, wearing his boxer briefs from yesterday. That man had a killer body. A smile curved onto her cheeks, and she stared. In a million years, this wouldn't have been the way she pictured her first morning in her temporary apartment.

He must've felt her gaze because he stopped and turned to her. *That face, whoa, and that chest...* There was a reason he'd always made those magazine lists and, for as long as she'd known him, never had a problem finding a date.

He covered the phone. "You okay? Talk to Sugar?"

"Calling." She shook the phone in her hand but went to the kitchenette to see if a furnished apartment came with food.

He went back to pacing. "There's nothing to talk about. End of discussion. Move on."

Yeah, he was talking about the picture. Last night had been special for her and fun for him. But her mind started ticking. How could he date an actress who played a tassel- and glitter-wearing burlesque dancer and still win his upcoming election? She wasn't a campaign genius, but it seemed like bad public relations for him.

"There's nothing to address. Nothing to define. Can we get back to how the latest focus group reacted to whatever they reacted to? Don't you have some fundraiser I need to know about?" His fingers pinched the bridge of his nose, and he looked up.

Busted. She busied herself in an empty kitchen. Furnished apartments didn't come stocked with food. At least hers didn't.

Asher padded over, still only in his boxer briefs. Her sheet was still wrapped around her. They made quite the pair.

He whispered, "It's not a big deal. Don't look so worried."

She didn't believe him but nodded. "I'll call Sugar now." Because waking her up and dropping this bomb on her would be as much fun as listening to Asher talk about how there was nothing worth defining when it came to her.

SEVEN

Jenny rubbed her eyes and wished her duffel bag had made it to the apartment. Until she was able to get it, she had no face wash, no makeup, and no clean clothes.

But she did have her sister on the phone, and the familial inquisition was reaching a boiling point. Sugar said something to someone in the background. Jenny could only assume it was Jared, and why that made her uneasy, she couldn't pinpoint. Titan was just a little overwhelming. Some of Sugar's customers purchased antique pistols. Titan bulk-ordered special-order grenade launchers.

Sugar came back to the phone. "Walk me through this one more time, Jenny."

She sighed. "Okay—"

"Jenny." Jared had the phone now. Her brother-in-law wasn't scary until he was pissed off. Right about now, he sounded pissed. Probably not at her. But still, the scary attitude was loud and clear. "I'll have a team in New York to meet with you and McIntyre by the afternoon."

"I have rehearsals." And she had no idea why she said that lame-ass excuse, other than everyone starting to treat her like her life was really in danger made it seem... really in danger.

Jared laughed, but it sounded a little like a grumble. "A wannabe Special Forces nutcase takes a picture of you, and you think your rehearsals are going to slow my men down?"

"Um, no."

"Smart girl." Sugar said something in the background, but Jenny couldn't hear it. Jared continued, "So you and Asher McIntyre?"

Her cheeks burned. The whole world apparently wanted to ask that question, and she didn't really know what to say or what Asher thought. Like all of a sudden, it was a topic of conversation when she had barely come to grips with the man even wanting to kiss her. And that had been yesterday.

"Maybe. I don't know..."

...why I'm talking to Jared about Asher?

...how to respond to that question?

...what I hope Asher's answer to Jared's question would be?

There were a million ways she could finish that sentence. For as confident as she'd felt last night, this morning was a cold splash of uncertainties.

"McIntyre's not stupid. Neither are you. But if he hurts you, he'll never see Election Day."

Oh. "I, um..."

Jared laughed. "Looks like you got the older brother you never wished you had, kid. Blame Sugar."

Asher's call had ended, and he walked over to her. "That's Sugar?"

"Jared," she whispered.

Jared growled in her ear. "That McIntyre?"

"Yes," Jenny said into the phone. "He had me call you guys. Guess he was making sure I did it."

Jared grunted, but it sounded like an approving sound. "Guess not all politicians are morons. Until my boys show up, don't leave that man's side."

She watched Asher stretch as he walked back toward the bedroom. *No problem.*

•••

Asher kept an eye on Jenny while he sat with Ricky and two men who came from Titan. Roman and Rocco. They seemed like decent guys, though they had only arrived two minutes ago, and he hadn't felt them out yet. But Asher approved of their *give-me-a-reason-to-kill-you-* look and was a fan of anyone who walked in the door with a plan. No pleasantries. Just a *this is what we're going to do.*

Plus, Jenny had met them at Sugar's wedding reception. Judging by the men's demeanors, they were personally affronted that Maxwell had stepped inside their world and threatened someone they knew. Asher approved.

Rocco shifted in the theatre's auditorium chair. "So that's our plan. Ricky stays in place. We stay nearby after running through a few quick security measures. FBI tracks Maxwell down, and we'll all be home by the end of the week."

Ricky nodded to him. "Mr. Congressman." He twirled a string of sequins around his finger and snapped it at Asher's knee. "How might you be staying safe while all this is happening?"

He'd been waiting for Ricky to ask that. Murphy had asked as well when Asher had spoken with him earlier about Titan Group picking up the lead on Jenny's protective detail. She was a bigger target now that a few reports decreed her a "newsworthy flame."

"Flavor of the week," as some jerk blogger had said. Asher had given his pit bull of a press secretary the go-ahead to tear that asshole apart.

The phone he used for campaign work buzzed. The other cell phone he carried for official business did the same. Ricky's phone rang. They both looked away from the stage and to their phones. Rocco and Roman looked at them. The timing was odd.

The fire alarm blared. Roman and Rocco jumped up. Ricky stepped to Asher, no longer playing the acting-choreography coach but morphing into the well-trained man that Asher knew well.

His stomach sank. Impending disaster was striking. Both Titan men were taking several steps at a time down the theatre's aisle toward the practice stage. Actors had stopped on stage, and a few covered their ears. Crew members walked onto the stage. It was a cacophony of people in mass hysteria.

The fire sprinklers turned on overhead. The emergency lights lit, and stage lights died.

In the blinking lights and under the water pouring from the ceiling, smoke began to fill the stage. The smoke floated and swirled under the gyrating lights. The sirens were too loud to shout over.

People began to run and call for help. Someone slipped in the water.

One second, Asher could see Jenny blinking on stage under a strobe light. The next, his eyes caught a man on stage, mixed in with the crew, who focused on Jenny. The only person who wasn't reacting to the craziness.

"Maxwell!" Asher shouted and pointed to Ricky, to the Titan men who were jumping on stage.

He pushed his way out of his aisle to the stairs. An explosion sounded at the back of the theatre; the lights went black. An eruption of screams staggered through the theatre.

Two beams of light illuminated on the stage. Had to be Roman and Rocco. They flashed all directions, then the overhead lights came back on.

Jenny was gone.

Ricky hustled Asher down the stairs and opposite from Roman and Rocco. He struggled to head toward stage. "Get your hands off me."

"Move your ass, Ash."

"Damn it, Richard."

"Move. Outside. Let Titan handle Jenny. I need to get you secure."

"Me? Secure? Fuck that—"

"Deal I made with Murphy. Move your ass, Congressman."

Fuck Ricky and Murphy. He should've known, having dealt with FBI and private security too many times before. They would talk, make their own plans. Asher was the man they wanted to protect. The public official who the FBI wouldn't let down. "You fucking played me."

"No, brother. I didn't. But you bet your congressional pin that it's in my job duty to keep you safe as well."

They made it outside, completely soaked and stinking like a fog machine. Asher scrubbed his hands over his face, into his hair, furious. He paced in place. Glared at Richard. And he waited. Roman or Rocco would give them an update. Explain that they had killed Maxwell in the hallway. Something. Anything.

His phone rang, and he answered it on the first ring. "What?"

"Now there's something in play that we both want."

A chill ran down Asher's spine. He roared into the phone, but the line was dead.

•••

Jenny came to, soaking wet in a dark space. The hum of road noise and the occasional illumination of red lights along the back panel delivered the bad news. She was stuffed in a car trunk, wearing a practice costume. A black bustier, glittery boy shorts, and high heels that would make the burlesque world proud. Not the best run-and-escape outfit, and she sure wouldn't be blending into a crowd if she did get out in public.

Two immediate options popped to mind. Kick out a tail light and stick her foot out the trunk. That would surely get someone's attention. Or she could wait until they stopped somewhere and scream until a passerby heard and called for help.

She opted not to wait and began kicking. The tail light didn't budge. Not as easy as it looked on television. Every pothole and sharp turn jarred her. The air was warm and stuffy and seemed to worsen with each passing hour.

It had to be hours. Right? Where were they going?

Eternity passed, and finally the car stopped for longer than a red light. The engine cut off, and her stomach tightened. She might throw up.

But that wouldn't help her.

Get it together, Jenny!

She sucked down a weak breath and willed her nerves to quiet down. They only semi-listened. A lock clicked, and the trunk popped. She jumped up to the same man who'd offered to be her acting coach and who matched a photo Asher had shown her that morning. *Maxwell.*

"Why are you doing this?"

"Doesn't matter to you."

Jenny tried to scamper out of the trunk, but his thick arm caught her. She blinked under the pressure on her neck and threw her hands in the air. He would knock her out again. She remembered that was how he'd done it the first time.

"Sorry," she choked out. "Shouldn't have done that."

His arm released, and she looked around, for the first time realizing where they were. *I'm at home?* The car was parked in the alley behind her apartment. But why?

He dragged her to the back entrance and jimmied the door open then did the same to her apartment and walked in. The most comforting place in her whole world now appeared dark and menacing. The man kept the lights off and pushed her on to the couch.

"Stay."

She nodded. Would anyone think to look for her at home? What did he want with her? Too many questions flooded her mind. Her head pounded, her limbs trembled, but her stomach growled.

Maxwell looked at her. Guess her stomach growled loudly.

"Get up."

Jenny stood and wobbled in her heels.

"Kitchen." He directed her as if she didn't know where it might be. "Get some food."

"Okay."

His voice hadn't been nice, but the gesture was, and she didn't trust it. She could run better on bare feet and would as soon as the opportunity presented itself. Jenny slipped off her shoes in front of the fridge.

"Are you hungry?" she offered, the refrigerator door open. Make friends with the enemy. Sun Tzu said that kind of stuff, right? Molly always said things like that. Asher probably thought like that too.

The man grunted and stalked around the kitchen, checking out the window.

"Find food quickly and shut the door."

Jenny nodded. "I know you don't want to hurt me." He didn't answer but went to each window, placing wires and small blocks on each. "I won't tell a soul if you just walk out now. Please."

What were those things? Alarms? Mini-bombs?

He turned and narrowed his eyes. "Find something to eat."

She pulled a container of dip out of the fridge. "Sorry. Just trying to make conversation. I'm bad with quiet."

Really, she wasn't. She would prefer nothing more than silence and to be left alone. But that wasn't going to happen. So she would butter him up. He might let down his guard and make a mistake, and then she could escape. And if nothing else, maybe he'd let her throw on some jeans. Her legs were freezing in the glittery boy shorts.

Maxwell looked into the hall but stayed nearby. "Try to keep your mouth shut."

"Chips?" She grabbed a bag from the cabinet. "Sorry. Not supposed to talk. Got it."

Maybe if he thought of her as a friendly captive, he'd be less likely to kill her. Food seemed to work with most men. Chips and dip and good manners were the best options she could come up with.

"Sit down. Eat your chips." He handed her an envelope and a cell phone then walked out of the kitchen.

Her eyes went wide as she sat in the dark, ignoring the chips and dip. What was up with the phone? Was the note for her to read? If she made a call, would her building blow up? Confusion racked her brain. What was happening?

Jenny looked over her shoulder when the front door shut. *What is going on?*

Did he just leave her here? With a phone?

"Hello?" She pivoted in her seat, scared this was a trick or a test. "Excuse me, Mr. Maxwell?"

Silence.

She listened. *Nothing.* All this grief only to be taken home? She wanted to scream. Instead, she picked up the small envelope and held it toward the window like she would be able to read its contents. *Nothing to see.* She slipped her finger under the edge and opened it. Cardstock fell out.

Dear Congressman McIntyre,

I'm done watching and waiting. Now you know what it feels like when someone steals from you. Last chance, right your wrong. It's almost Election Day. Consider that your deadline.

Best wishes,

Maxwell

Maxwell had no intention of hurting her? He just wanted to scare Asher? Well, screw him.

EIGHT

Asher's phone had five percent charge left, which was more than he could say for his energy level. Hours passed like years. He had seceded control of his day to the FBI and his campaign team. And what little part remained his had been ramrodded by Molly, Sugar, Jared, and Titan. Asher's head spun, and he would've passed out, but that required too much energy.

The FBI and campaign had spun the incident as an unfortunate false alarm and failed fire safety system. No mention of Jenny's kidnapping. They wanted to keep her out of the public's eye for any number of reasons that Asher didn't agree with. The FBI insisted it was safer for her, and his campaign consultants had no problem with that.

The only problem was he did, and not a single person listened to a thing he said. If anyone ever accused him of having power and using his influence to get his way, Asher would laugh to the brink of insanity. Because that was where he was now—on the verge of losing his mind. So exhausted and drained that he could barely function, yet unable to close his eyes or walk away in case something turned up.

His phone rang. The number came up unknown. Maybe Maxwell was in the mood to talk. Asher needed a cell phone charger if that was the case.

He accepted the call. "Yeah. McIntyre."

"Ash."

"Jenny?" Relief washed over him. Asher could finally take a deep breath. "Where are you? Are you okay? What—"

"I'm in DC. At home, by myself—"

Asher waved his arm. Someone had to be paying attention to him. A kid of an agent walked over. Maybe an intern. Didn't matter. "Find Murphy. Jenny's at home. And get an update to Jared at Titan. Now." He took a breath and said a thanksgiving prayer. "You're okay? Are you hurt? Are you alone?" So many questions rushed out of his mouth.

"I think I'm okay."

"You're whispering."

"He just left me here. I don't understand. I'm scared it's a trick. There are things on the windows. But he gave me this phone and a note."

"What's on the window?"

"I don't know. Wires. Blocks. Stickers."

"Don't touch a thing. Sit still and don't touch anything. Do you understand?" He covered the phone and jumped toward the kid he'd sent to find Murphy. "Send a bomb squad and get me a cell phone charger." He checked his phone. The red light flashed. "Sweetheart, if I lose you, I'll call you back in a minute. Where are you calling me from?"

"The phone Maxwell left me."

No. What if it was rigged to explode when she hung up? Another agent ran over with a phone charger. He plugged in and was given an update that Titan was tapping into the line. *Now that was something that Titan could do off the books that a federal agency couldn't touch without a year's worth of paperwork.*

A minute later, Jared joined the call. He walked her through a series of questions, and by the time he was done, the bomb squad was at Jenny's door. A nuclear attack couldn't have gotten Asher off that call. After this debacle was said and done, he was going to find Jared Westin and shake his hand. Jared had kept Jenny collected and evaluated the situation.

Titan's opinion was the setup on the window was a complete middle finger to the congressman. Jared's language had been more colorful, and Asher liked the guy more and more. But what he didn't like was a confirmation that Maxwell Bowie knew what he was doing and wanted to show off. He had set up several explosives and charges but hadn't armed a single one. It was strictly a look-at-what-could-have-happened move.

The bomb squad confirmed everything that Jared had figured out over the phone, and damn if Asher wasn't impressed. They took the phone Maxwell had given her into evidence. Jenny said she would finagle a new one and call him back after talking to Sugar.

He used that quick minute to make arrangements for a private charter to DC. He would have Jenny in his arms tonight, no matter what he had to do.

His phone rang again. Again, he didn't know the number but knew it was her. "I'll be there in a few hours."

"Awesome." She sounded exhausted. "But there's a hundred people in my living room."

"Then I'll make one hundred and one."

"I wasn't saying I didn't want you to come over."

He could hear her smile, and it warmed his heart. "Get some sleep, sweetheart."

A heavy pause hung on the line. "Ash?"

"Yeah?"

"I'm glad you're coming here."

He nodded. "Nothing could keep me away."

Silence still hung on the phone. He didn't want to hang up. It killed him to be so far away.

"Ash?"

His chest ached, and he wanted to hold her. Kiss her. Make everything better. "We've had a crazy couple of days. Whatever's on your mind, you can say it now, say it later. Just know I'm coming for you. I've known you most my life, sweetheart, and I'm an ass that it's taken me this long to figure it out: I need you. I crave you. You're a requirement to function. Take that for what it's worth, and I'll wake you up when I get there."

"I—"

"I will see you soon enough. Sleep tight." Whatever was on her mind could be said to his face.

•••

The sunshine shone through her windows when Jenny woke. She smiled. Asher was under the covers and had cradled her into the crook of his arm. How could she not have awakened when he arrived? When he'd taken off his shirt and slipped under the covers?

She smiled even bigger. And how was it possible that Asher McIntyre was asleep past the break of dawn? Maybe she was rubbing off on him.

Her hand drew lazy circles under the blanket and over his stomach. "Good morning."

He shifted and tightened his arm over her shoulder. "Careful. That's a dangerous way to wake a man."

She giggled and flattened her palm, sliding to the waistband of his boxers. "What? Saying good morning seems harmless enough."

He covered her roving hand and moved it over him. "Your pleasantries weren't what I was talking about."

Asher's mind might have been waking up, but the rest of him was raring to go. He hooked his other arm over her back and brought her to lie on him, legs straddling him. Jenny rested her cheek on his chest, and his lips pressed to the top of her head.

"I was scared I lost you, sweetheart." He kissed the top of her head again then flipped them over. His jawline had a rough shadow, and his perfect hair was messy. Asher's gaze burned through her until he broke and kissed her tenderly. "Lots of things have been put in perspective now."

"Like?" Her throat ached from saying one simple word. There was so much that could be hanging on that question.

"You."

"Oh." She bit her lip, unsure what to say. "Meaning?"

"It means..." His forehead dipped against hers. "It means I've always cared about you. Always wondered how you'd taste and what would make you scream." He kissed her lips. "I never let myself wonder..."

Her heart raced. "About?"

"Anything but me. Selfish politician, huh?" He chuckled softly. "But now I'm wondering what you want. If you want me. If you want to make love."

She nodded as her world spun. He could love her in any way, and it would be amazing.

Asher kissed her, deeper and longer. His tongue probed her mouth, but then he softened the intensity. His eyes blazed. "I need to know if you have that same ache that's been plaguing me."

"For far too long." Her heart banged in her chest, and she slipped off her panties. His boxer-covered erection flexed against her mound.

"God, I need you, Jenny. *Need.*"

"You do?" Jenny snagged his boxers and pushed them over his bottom, and he took care of them the rest of the way down. The thick emotional tension that hung on their words made it hard to breathe, even as it cocooned them together. She needed him too, in more ways than she could describe.

"My head, my heart, they're both saying the same thing. I love you, sweetheart, and I have for a long time from a distance."

Her heart sang. Fireworks exploded in her mind. It was everything she'd ever wanted to hear, and their lips met. A touch. A kiss. A confirmation. "I love you too. Have since I probably shouldn't have."

"There's nothing more I want to do"—he reached for his wallet, removed a condom, and sheathed himself—"than hear you say that again."

Asher pressed against her sex, and her eyes closed. "I love you."

He inched in then out. Kissing her. Holding her. Jenny wrapped arms and legs around him and let him work them both together. He was thick. Forceful, but still taking his time.

Asher explored her mouth. His hands caressed her curves. They moved as one. Breaths interchanged, interweaved. His heart beat against her breasts. His scratchy cheek rasped her neck, and hot breaths crawled across her skin.

Perfect pressure and precision. Wrapped into his embrace, she'd given herself over to him completely. He owned her body, even if he didn't know it. But he did know she loved him, that he loved her. That magnitude hit with each stroke and drive. His words burned into her memory. She could recall them forever; that she knew.

Jenny caught his mouth, bit his lip, and a tornado of bliss swept her into a frenzy. Her muscles clenched; a climax so deep and emotional wracked through her. Her sex spasmed, and her hopes exploded.

"I love you." She moaned while she came. She cried his name, and he stole her breath, finishing with her. Asher collapsed over her, and they lay, spent, connected, together on so many levels.

Drifting to sleep, he said it again. "I love you too."

NINE

Six weeks later

The lights and the crowd were enough to make Asher hot under the collar. As were the impending election results. He'd gone into Election Day knowing that polling and nightly tracking were on his side. But, despite what his consultants said, there was always the chance that voters wouldn't behave as they should. Asher didn't trust that he was a shoo-in.

He didn't trust anything today. Today was Maxwell's deadline, and Asher hadn't heard a thing from the man since Jenny had been abducted and released. Even if he had, he wouldn't negotiate through threats, and he had no control over the highway expansion or government's claim of eminent domain that had seized the Bowie Estate.

The FBI hadn't found any sign of Maxwell. The silence ate at his nerves, and he tried to trust in his resources. Titan had focused on Jenny. She'd been under constant surveillance. They handled her transportation between Washington and New York and oversaw security for *Tassels and Tangos.*

Jenny was flustered by Titan's attention, even if they blended into the background. She was also amazed by the response from her new fans. Life had changed quickly with the massive success of *Tassels and Tangos*—fan mail, phone calls for interviews, and an agent who returned her e-mails—but Jenny hadn't changed at all.

Asher looked at her talking to a woman outside a polling location. Jenny gave the woman's kid a *McIntyre for Senate* balloon and sticker, and the little kid squealed. Asher knew Titan had eyes on her as well, but he was hesitant every time Jenny stopped to talk to someone. It was only a matter of time before Maxwell struck.

Once they made it through the day, he had a big surprise for her, and he couldn't wait.

Jenny waved to the kid and walked over, taking Asher's hand. "Ready to go? Polls close in five minutes, and that was the last stop before we head to your party." She swung his hand and smiled brightly. "Come on. Don't be so serious. Everything is fine."

She was confident in his win and had ignored the looming threat. She had gone on and on about not wanting to bring him down on his big day.

Elections results aren't my concern. You are. Asher looked around and didn't see the undercover security detail, only Murphy, who had been traveling with them on each campaign stop.

"Let's do this." He nodded, and Murphy moved toward their waiting vehicle.

With a quick wave to reporters who were manning the precinct location, he got into the back seat with Jenny and gave her a kiss.

They rode to the hotel in silence. His campaign team had their war room set up in one of the suites. He'd been in elections enough to know what it looked like. A mobile command center. Interns and staff. Several computer monitors set up on desks and makeshift tables. His campaign manager and consultants geared up for precinct-level data to float in. His press team had charged cell phones and laptops ready with pre-written press releases.

They arrived at the back entrance and took the stairs to the campaign's suite. Downstairs in a ballroom was a crowd of volunteers, voters, and reporters. There was probably music blasting and an open bar. A few large screens showing the live feed from news stations. Normally, all this would psych him up, but Asher wanted nothing to do with crowds. Nothing to do with anything that might endanger Jenny.

His campaign consultant smiled and gave a big thumbs-up. "Early numbers are in. You killed in the swing counties. Locked up your voters. I give it two minutes tops before the AP calls it for you."

Asher nodded, and his phone rang. The shrill sound made his stomach drop. He could feel the blood rush out of his face. He pulled his phone out and didn't know the number.

"McIntyre."

"Congratulations, Senator McIntyre." The voice was familiar and welcome. His opponent.

Asher cleared his throat and tried to wipe away the panic that had quickly gurgled up. "Thank you for a hard-fought race." They made the necessary small talk, but he watched Jenny. She was itching to get out of the suite and join the party.

He ended the call. The press team was already notifying reporters that his opponent had called to concede. Breaking news flashed across several television screens—McIntyre Wins New York's Senate Seat.

The room erupted into applause and congratulations. A video monitor of the victory party in the ballroom showed the same thing.

He turned to Murphy. "Walk me through the security again."

"We've swept the room. Everyone's passed through metal detectors. Titan is in the ballroom. We've got eyes on the reporters, hotel staff, and crowd."

"Maxwell is here. I know he is."

"Might be, Senator."

Asher gave Murphy a look. Only within the last week had the agent been convinced to stop calling Asher "Congressman."

He turned to Jenny. "I want you on stage with me." Out of arm's reach wasn't acceptable.

Her jaw dropped. "That's like a family and staff thing."

His family couldn't make it. Molly was working election night in Washington, and his parents both had the flu and had called him obsessively all day. Besides, Jenny was family. That was a conversation he would bring up soon. Until then, a simple explanation would have to suffice. "I need you by my side."

She beamed. "Let's do this!"

•••

Asher's paranoid mood frazzled Jenny's nerves, but she had no intention of showing that reaction. She'd decided early on, it was better to be all smiles and support than it was to feed into the tension. They both knew Maxwell would make an appearance. Titan knew it. The FBI knew it.

She tugged at her shirt and felt like she'd been Velcroed into a straight jacket. Both the FBI and Titan insisted that both she and Asher wear Kevlar vests. There was no sugarcoating their concerns after that request had been made mandatory. None of the men appreciated the challenges of finding a shirt and jacket that worked while wearing a bulletproof vest. Not that looks were an issue. Staying alive was the obvious goal. But still, a little more notice would have been helpful.

Asher took her hand as they walked into the ballroom, and her stomach fluttered. The room erupted in cheers. The music blasted. Cameras jumped in their faces. She grinned until her cheeks hurt and watched Asher, the picture of cool under pressure.

A million butterflies spun circles in her stomach while her hand went clammy in his grip.

"Doing okay, sweetheart?"

"Of course." That might have been the first lie she'd ever told him. She went on tiptoes to his ear and whispered, "Just more attention than I'm used to."

Their relationship wasn't a secret. Reporters loved the up-and-coming-actress-tames-playboy-politician storyline.

"Get used to it. They're all here for you. I'm just the story they have to report on." He tugged her close. "I love you."

They made their way to the big donors. Asher said his spiel to each of them, shaking hands and exchanging hugs. People she didn't know squeezed her shoulder and offered *her* congratulations. *I wasn't the one who did anything.*

He nodded out of a conversation and put his arm around her waist. "You're going to do great."

"And I once had a performance review that said I couldn't smile and walk at the same time. Look at me go."

Asher laughed and kissed her. The crowd clapped and cheered. Photographers' cameras popped. The bright flashes were blinding. She blinked, trying to keep her bearings. So many people, and the room was so warm. They all crushed against her and Asher. She hung on to his hand, letting him lead her.

Jenny tried to look for Maxwell. Tried to pinpoint Titan and the FBI. She failed all around. Faces closed in on her from every direction. Well wishes were shouted at Asher. He climbed a flight of stairs, bringing her along in hand. At the top of the platform, the music changed again. The screens behind him spun red, white, and blue graphics. Spotlights began to gyrate as the lights went down.

The FBI had told her what would happen. But knowing and experiencing were two different things. She'd been onstage hundreds of times. But this was different. This was different from even the rallies and campaign stops they'd made leading up to election night. This was political pandemonium, and she'd always been a vaguely interested participant who supported the McIntyre family. She'd never been under this kind of limelight.

Asher raised their joined arms, and the room exploded in applause. He took a step back, giving her a nod and a grin before he pulled her into another kiss. The lip lock quieted the room, until he pulled back, and there was everyone else, louder than before.

With his arm around her, he gave her a hug and whispered, "You're amazing. A pro. Soon as the speech is done, we're out of here."

She nodded. Smiled. Stepped to the side like she had been instructed to, so he could take the podium in front of the teleprompter. Asher was an orator. He didn't need the screens to tell him what to say, but over the weeks, she'd realized he used them to stay on track.

"Thank you, New York State." Cheers and applause thundered. Lights flashed. "I couldn't have done this without you. The volunteers and voters who made this night happen..."

Jenny watched as he moved through the rehearsed words. She'd memorized it too. Knew when people would laugh. Expected when the crowd would nod. It was almost over. She and Asher stood on a stage, sitting like targets for Maxwell. But nothing.

Asher delivered his final line, and it was a home run, as she'd known it would be. The crowd began to chant. The balloons fell. Hundreds. Maybe thousands of patriotic-colored balloons fell from the ceiling. Silver, shimmering confetti mixed in. The lights blinked and flashed a spectacular light show.

She couldn't breathe. Couldn't see. And Asher was on her arm again, leading her through the crowd.

Congratulations and shouts of support began all over again. The crowd overwhelmed her. People stepped on her shoes. Clapped on her back. Said things to her like they were old friends. And then the familiar face of Maxwell Bowie was inches from her nose. Smiling. Clapping. Reaching for her.

"Asher!"

He faced the other direction, still holding on to her hand. Her grip tightened, and her nails dug into his flesh. Everything turned to slow motion. Her words became heavy and slow. Asher turned, like in the movies, but her hand fell away. Hard hands took her elbows, and she was off her feet and moving away from Asher. Away from Maxwell.

"Move. Move. Move." The voice bellowed from behind her.

Rocco. Titan.

"Asher!" Why had Rocco pulled them apart?

A collective gasp rolled behind her. Chaos and confusion bubbled. She tried to turn her head and see what was happening. The overhead lights turned on. And the music stopped. She could hear people rushing out of the room. What the hell was happening?

As Rocco rounded a corner, she could see several men piled together, as if they'd been tackling Maxwell or protecting Asher. Or guarding him? Had he been hurt? What had Maxwell done?

Jenny thrashed in Rocco's arms. "Let me go! Where's Ash?"

They entered a hallway behind the stage, and he carried her to a back room. Finally, he put her down, and she turned, ready to scream. Rocco's face had blood on it. His shoulder. His hands.

"Christ," he growled, scrutinizing his arm, then flicked his wrist to his mouth. "Tassels is secure." Blood poured down his arm, and he dropped it.

She'd only heard them reference her codename once. But the ridiculousness of it paled in comparison to Rocco's arm wound. "You need help. Tell them you're hurt."

He growled and felt around on his chest. "Does hurt like a mother bear, that's for sure."

Rocco's breaths wheezed. Was it his chest too? God, there was a lot of blood. "You need help."

"Not a chance."

She looked at the floor. Blood stains pooled at his feet. There was way more blood coming off him than he either realized or would admit. "Call someone on your mic piece and tell them you're hurt."

He shook his head. "Orders are we do not move until we get the all clear."

"Dang it, Rocco." Stubborn men. "Then where's Asher? What happened?"

"It's fine. Hang tight."

Rocco hadn't said *he's fine.* And *why* was Rocco bleeding? She hadn't heard an explosion, no gunshot. "What about you? What happened?"

"Knife slice. Just need a few dozen stitches, and I'll be fine." He laughed and grimaced. "Oh, fuck me."

"What's wrong?"

"Don't feel right."

"You've lost too much blood."

"No. Something else. Fuckin' dizzy." He took a deep breath, and his eyes unfocused. "I know blood… loss. Not it." He scrubbed his hand over his face. His brow furrowed, and he stared at his arm, the blood. "Damn. It. Jenny," he slurred. "Hallucinations."

He started to disarm. One gun off his hip. Another off his leg. A holstered knife.

“Take them. Now.” Rocco leaned against the door. He pressed his mic to his mouth. “Knife wound. Poisoned. Tassels is unguarded.”

“I’m *what*?” Guns she was comfortable with. The knife, not so much. She stuck that in her pocket, tucked his compact Glock into her waistband, and kept the Smith & Wesson pistol in hand.

He batted his hand in front of his face as if swooshing away flies. “Fucking. Seeing shit.” He flinched. And again. “Get out of here.”

“Where should I go?” What had happened out there? She had to find Asher. Or maybe Jared or Murphy. Roman was out there too. Any of them could help Rocco and confirm Asher was fine. Someone would point her in the right direction. A cop or an agent. She was the senator’s girlfriend. That had to help her get where she needed to go and have her questions answered.

Rocco slumped out of the way, twitching.

“I’ll get help.”

•••

“Enough already.” Asher shook off Murphy and Roman. “You got that fucker?”

They were in a large, loud boiler room adjacent to the ballroom.

Murphy nodded. “He’s in custody.”

“The plan wasn’t to separate me from Jenny unless—” *someone was hurt.* He blinked. “Where’s Jenny?”

Jared hung up the phone and motioned to Roman and Murphy. “We have a problem. Let’s go.”

“Was she hurt?” Asher growled into Jared’s face.

“No. Rocco got in front of the blade. Took it to the arm and chest.”

Asher could’ve felt like a bastard that he was relieved but didn’t care. “Where is she?”

“That’s the problem.”

“Explain the problem to me, so help me God.”

“Knife must’ve been tainted, treated with a psychotic. Rocco called it in as he started hallucinating. We found security footage. A cop escorted Maxwell *onto* the property and into the ballroom.”

Asher’s mind raced. “There’s a second man?”

"Roger that, Senator." Jared headed to the door. "Roman, get to Rocco. Murphy, check in with your men. We've sent a screenshot and description for you to distribute."

Jared and Roman left. Murphy picked up his phone and began issuing orders. *Screw this.* Asher walked out and went to find his girl.

He rounded corners and walked through a labyrinth of corridors. He tried her cell phone. No answer. Not a single cop or agent could be trusted, and he wished he'd seen the picture of the second man. Too late now.

At the end of the hallway, he came to a T. Roman and Jared might have split up. They might have known where Rocco had been and headed directly there. Asher went right. He had no reason. His phone rang. *Murphy.* Click and he sent the guy to voice mail. Murphy redialed him, and Asher was moving to find Jenny. No time to explain that he wouldn't be cooped up in a boiler room.

He rounded another corner. *Jenny!* And she was holding a gun? "Sweetheart."

She was walking with a cop who looked trustworthy, but Asher didn't trust anyone. Jenny smiled, started toward him. Just as fast, the cop snaked an arm around her waist. *Son of a bitch.*

Jenny's face screwed. Confusion and panic tore at her cheeks. Only twenty-five yards between them, but the distance suddenly felt like a mile.

"Let her go. You want me. You want to talk about the Bowie place, that's fine. Let's talk. Let her go."

The cop shucked the gun out of her hand. "You should have taken my brother seriously."

A brother? How had this not been realized before? Asher stepped toward them. "Fine. My mistake. Not hers."

"Like Max said, we lost something of ours. This is all about her and making sure you know how it feels to lose something."

Ten feet was all that remained between them. "You won't make it past me."

"You and who else, asshole? Everyone's running around pointing fingers at each other. No one knows who the dirty cop is."

Jenny ripped her arm free and behind her. A gun clattered to the floor, and she kicked and pushed at it with her high heels. Asher dove for it as the other man raised a gun at him. He heard Jenny grunt, kick, and scream. A shot rang out, the ricocheting bullet pinging around Asher but not hitting. He had Jenny's Glock. Who knew where she'd found two guns? Didn't matter. Asher had aimed, and Jenny struggled in the Bowie brother's arm. Her arms flayed, and she pulled a knife from her pocket, slashing at the man's arm around her.

The Bowie brother hollered, releasing her, and Asher ran forward, punched him, relishing the snap of his jaw. Jenny dove behind Asher, and he pounced on the downed man, whipping him across the face with the gun. Bowie Brother was out cold.

Asher took a deep breath and turned to Jenny. Her eyes were wide, but she wasn't bleeding and didn't look hurt. "Sweetheart?"

She nodded.

"You okay?"

She nodded again.

He pulled his phone out of his pocket and redialed Murphy. "Now you owe me, and I never want to hear 'sir' again."

•••

It was the middle of the night. The lights and sirens had long since disappeared. Titan and the FBI were gone. The news vans were even packing up after the crazy night of on-air reporting.

Asher watched Jenny finish the last of the cake they'd ordered from room service. He made a mental note to thank them for scrounging it up even after the kitchen had closed.

"Talk about a night we're going to remember." She tossed the fork onto the crumb-covered plate. "That was good. Chocolate makes everything better."

"Did you think we'd ever be here?" he asked.

"Snacking on room service while naked in bed after your stalkers tried to kill us? Nope." She giggled. "But I could at least have imagined the naked and cake thing."

"Think you want to do this next election night?"

"Heck yeah."

"What about the one after that?"

She laughed and stretched next to him. "I'm pretty sure you can coax me anywhere with a good piece of cake."

"What if I wanted to be governor?"

She smiled. "What if you want to be president?"

"You'd make a great first lady."

"Glad you think so. Let me know if anyone else is in the running. I've apparently got some great fighting moves I might try out again."

He laughed and pulled her against his chest. "What if I wanted to walk away from it all after this term? I'd be some normal guy with a famous actress on his arm."

"No one's famous but you."

"You keep telling yourself that, and one of these days you'll realize the truth."

She shrugged. "What if we were both unknown?"

"I'd still love you like crazy." He kissed her. "And I'd still want you by my side."

"Good."

He rolled off the bed and rummaged through his pants pocket. With a diamond ring in his hand, he watched Jenny's jaw drop. "I don't want you to remember tonight because of what happened earlier."

She closed her mouth and looked at him.

"Didn't think it would go the way it did. And I was going to wait until after tonight. Fancy dinner. Lots of roses. But I can't wait another minute. I need you to know that I'm in this forever. That I can't wait to marry you, whether we walk away from the spotlight or dive head first into something bigger. Whatever happens, I want you there as my wife. Jenny Chase, will you marry me?"

He took her hand and slid on the ring.

"Chocolate cake and a diamond ring? In bed with the man of my dreams?" She leaned over and kissed him. "Nothing else to say but yes."

THE END

ABOUT THE AUTHOR

Cristin Harber is a USA Today bestselling romantic suspense and military romance author. She lives outside Washington, DC with her family and English bulldog, and enjoys chatting with readers.

Facebook: www.facebook.com/CristinHarberauthor
Twitter: www.twitter.com/CristinHarber
Website: www.CristinHarber.com
Email: Cristin@CristinHarber.com
Newsletter: Stay in touch about all things Titan—releases, excerpts, and more—plus new series info. http://bit.ly/11aWFzM

Made in United States
Troutdale, OR
03/03/2024